THE SHADOW IN THE GALLERY

A Tale of the Smith Institute

By Thomas A. Christie

THE
STIRLING
SMITH

Other Books by
Thomas A. Christie

Liv Tyler: Star in Ascendance

The Cinema of Richard Linklater

John Hughes and Eighties Cinema:
Teenage Hopes and American Dreams

Ferris Bueller's Day Off:
The Pocket Movie Guide

The Christmas Movie Book

The James Bond Movies of the Eighties

Notional Identities: Ideology, Genre and
National Identity in Popular Scottish Fiction
Since the Seventies

CROWDFUNDING DEDICATIONS

This book could not have been produced without the kind contributions of the following individuals, all of whom generously supported the project during an international crowdfunding campaign operated by the Stirling Smith in 2013. Sincere and grateful thanks are due to each and every one.

This novel is dedicated to, and supported by:

The Provost, Baillies and the People of Stirling
The Gordon Fraser Charitable Trust
Chris Boyce
John and Sadie Canning
Dawn Elizabeth Chinery
Michael Donnelly
Scott Jordan
Elspeth King
Anne & Len McGuire
David, Christine & Jennifer Paterson
Sheila Pitcairn of Dunfermline
Anne Stewart OBE
David Smith
Rory Watson

For details of more people who helped to bring *The Shadow in the Gallery* to life, please also see the dedications at the back of the book.

First published in Great Britain in 2013 by The Stirling Smith Art Gallery and Museum.

A CIP catalogue record for this book is available from the British Library.

ISBN-10: 0-9546511-7-0
ISBN-13: 978-0-9546511-7-6

Typeset in Bookman Old Style.
Printed and bound in Great Britain by Martins, Seaview Works, Spittal, Berwick-upon-Tweed, TD15 1RS.

Cover illustration and design by Bill Botten.

Published by
The Stirling Smith Art Gallery and Museum
Dumbarton Road, Stirling, FK8 2RQ
A Registered Scottish Charity, SCO16162
www.smithartgalleryandmuseum.co.uk

FLOOR PLAN
OF THE SMITH INSTITUTE
IN THE LATE 19TH CENTURY

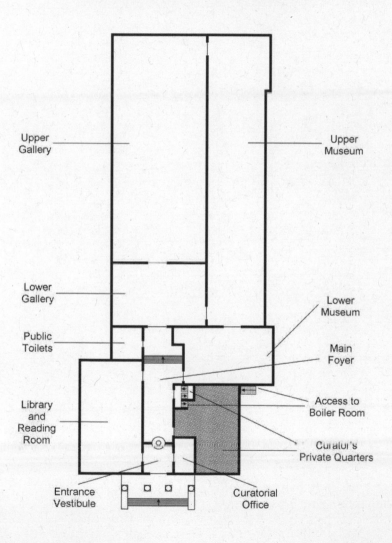

Upper
Gallery

Upper
Museum

Lower
Gallery

Lower
Museum

Public
Toilets

Main
Foyer

Library
and
Reading
Room

Access to
Boiler Room

Curator's
Private Quarters

Entrance
Vestibule

Curatorial
Office

The Smith Institute

Mr Alexander Croall (1804-1885)

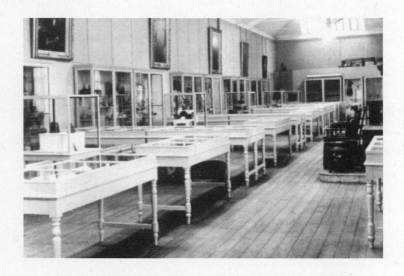

Upper Museum of the Smith Institute

Upper Gallery of the Smith Institute

CONTENTS

THE SHADOW IN THE GALLERY

A Tale of the Smith Institute

By Thomas A. Christie

www.theshadowinthegallery.co.uk

This book is dedicated to

Mrs Margaret Job

A good friend to me,
and to the Smith Institute.

August 1914

PROLOGUE
Of Times Gone By

It was quiet in the Smith Institute that day. There was a stillness in the early afternoon air that James Sword more readily associated with his nightly rounds; that discomfiting feeling he sometimes had when wandering through the deserted galleries and sensing the eyes of a particular portrait's subject bearing down upon him. At times he almost sensed that those intricate patterns of oil on canvas were watching his every move: bygone figures from history peering back at him from across the ages. That sensation came all but rarely these days; twenty-nine years as the Institute's curator had largely rid him of such fanciful notions, not least as the boundary between home and workplace had long since blurred into obscurity.

Home. The Smith didn't feel much like anyone's home these days. The brightness of the late summer sunshine reflected through the building's huge windows only seemed to emphasise the unsettling hush that permeated the now-emptied public areas. The Institute was not by nature accustomed to silence. Over the years Sword had grown used to the polite chatter of visitors, the amiable discourse of his staff and the laughter of children in the museum - including that of his own offspring, in years gone by.

But if there is one constant in life, it is change. His footfalls resonating with irregular audibility as he stepped out from the lower gallery onto the broad Caithness flagstones of the Smith's entry hallway, the curator was uncomfortably reminded of the reason for the deserted building's current woes. With the ringing out of a single shot in faraway Sarajevo less than two months ago, a spark had ignited a tinderbox in Europe, sending the continent hurtling towards an uncertain destiny. The assassination of the Archduke Franz Ferdinand had seen nation after nation stumbling towards martial mobilisation, with Britain declaring war on Germany and Austria mere weeks ago. For Stirling, a garrison town, the influence of the international climate had been immediate: Sword had never known activity at the Castle to be heightened to the degree that had been witnessed over the summer as enlistment had begun. But it was not the troops' preparations high on the ancient basalt crag that concerned him; this new wave of bellicose commotion had suddenly come much closer to Sword's area of jurisdiction than that.

The War Office had maintained authority over Stirling Castle since the beginning of the previous century, and Sword - like so many others of the area who professed an interest in history - had heard many accounts of the military renovation of the one-time royal stronghold of the Stuart dynasty. With the Chapel Royal having been converted into a dining hall, and the Palace itself now functioning as an officers' mess, Sword had often breathed a sigh of relief that the reach of the military zeal for practical refurbishment had not reached beyond the confines of the Castle walls. No clearer testament to this could be found than the infamous Stirling Heads - intricately carved wooden roundels which had only narrowly been salvaged from the imposing mediaeval citadel - which now adorned the Smith's natural history room in plaster-cast form, as had been the case since the building had opened to the public so many years ago.

Yet more inanimate eyes staring accusatorily at him as his solitary form stalked the building, the Heads looked down upon Sword from what had once been a reading room - though it now seemed difficult to believe that the ornately-ceilinged area had held a library in times past, its abundant contents having been transferred across town to the new McFarlane building scarcely a decade beforehand. Denuded of its exhibits, these days the room seemed as empty and neglected as a deserted old barn, save for the disconcerting plasterwork faces gazing down forlornly upon his position. But the curator felt entirely undeserving of their interred reproach. Though the whispers of the past seemed to haunt him in every corner of the evacuated galleries, he knew that this building had been founded on the belief that history should always be allowed the respect it deserved.

At least until now.

Sword had not been completely surprised to receive the requisition order from the War Office, authorised with the terse pen-stroke of some faceless Whitehall mandarin who doubtless would have struggled to find Stirling on a map (the days of the late Sir Henry Campbell-Bannerman now seeming impossibly far removed). But the confirmation of the harsh reality had been an unpleasant sensation nonetheless. The Smith's exhibition space remained the largest in Scotland's entire Central Belt - a fact that had clearly not gone unnoticed by someone in authority. With the outbreak of war, the Argyll and Sutherland Highlanders' still-swelling numbers had necessitated drastic action. Additional service battalions were already in the process of being assembled for General Kitchener's purposes, and these troops had to be billeted somewhere - an unavoidable reality of life in a town so wedded to military life as this one. The Smith was to be converted into a barracks, a training area, a manufacturing site for uniforms and the like. 'After all,' the Regimental Colonel had told him briskly a few short weeks ago, 'you must surely agree that none of us desire to see the Kaiser's men traversing Dumbarton Road.'

Suddenly feeling each and every one of his advancing years with painful immediacy, Sword found it difficult to know what was worse: the fact that the Institute's collections

4

were being systematically dismantled with little care as to their value and significance, or that he was being forced to watch as it happened. He and his wife Margaret had been allowed to remain resident in their living quarters within the building, as had his dear mother-in-law Mary, but only with the explicit understanding that they would not interfere with military affairs. The Smith and its grounds, he was already tired of hearing, must now be considered a military installation under the auspices of the armed services. His role - as custodian of the artefacts stored in the building - technically remained unchanged, he had been assured. But this seemed a rather less edifying prospect when almost every item was now stored away in cardboard boxes and wooden crates, with a seemingly endless array of fine artwork now in the process of being crammed into a far corner of the building to allow the army craftsmen ample room to complete their work on rather more utilitarian pursuits.

It was with some trepidation that Sword stepped through the doorway from the entrance hall into a darkened area that had, until recently, served as the Institute's lower museum. Although the room was graced by large windows which normally provided ample light, the sheer height of the stacked crates and mothballed storage cases which had been crammed along the external wall lent the space a rather dingy, cramped aspect that he could not fail to find oppressive. Along the opposing wall, row upon row of paintings were in evidence, stacked high upon a makeshift rack. Each had been hastily removed from their frames and rolled up with as much care as time had allowed him, as he had systematically stripped the walls of each gallery over the past weeks. Now devoid of its usual surfeit of vibrant colour provided by the various watercolours and oil paintings, the exhibition area today appeared little more than an empty warehouse, the unadorned walls awaiting the imminent arrival of wooden bunks for troops and work tables for seamstresses. Sporadic work had been underway in the upper gallery for weeks now, and the curator knew all too well that once the fruits of the army craftsmen's labour started to spill out into the rest of the building, it would seem all but unrecognisable in relation to its original form.

Sighing heavily, Sword eased himself down onto a crate that had been stacked next to the room's fireplace. How long before that old grate would see coal again, he wondered idly to himself, knowing that a roaring fire and an area packed full of rare and eminently combustible materials was seldom a good combination - least of all when necessity meant that an entire museum was being confined to a single room. Piled together in neat stacks around him were the few remaining unpacked items from this erstwhile treasure trove of ethnographic exhibits. He felt his bones creak as he tried to make himself comfortable on the makeshift seat. Although his dark, saturnine features had aged well with the passing years, the same could regrettably not be said for his joints, and though he had retained the rangy physicality of his youth his reactions were regrettably not what they had once been. This was a fact that caused him no end of frustration in recent years, not least given the sheer effort he had put into etching out a reputation as one of Scotland's most active museum curators in the decades gone by. With a rueful smile he cast his eyes across to a selection of stout boxes, knowing that the nondescript pile of containers held the entirety of the Institute's natural history collections. How many expeditions had he embarked upon over the years, he mused, his faithful gun-dog Bob never far from his side. Could the stewards of the National Museum's collections honestly claim to have played quite so direct a part in the acquisitions of their own holdings? Those innocuous cardboard storage boxes held everything from birds to butterflies, each one carefully preserved for the viewing pleasure of future generations. But even poor Bob had a touch of arthritis these days, and - much like the weary custodian himself - his physical responses were beginning to suffer for it.

'I can see that you have been productive, Mr Sword.'

The calm but authoritative voice seemed to come from nowhere and everywhere at once, momentarily startling the reflective curator. Sword turned to regard the new arrival with surprise, annoyed at himself for having been so obviously taken aback by the unexpected appearance. The newcomer was a stocky, well-groomed officer in regimental regalia; his epaulettes indicated his rank of Captain. An immaculate Glengarry bonnet was perched neatly upon his head, a swagger stick tucked smartly under his left arm. The young officer's features were open and pleasing, his cordiality seeming somewhat at odds with the austerity of his official attire. His bespectacled eyes, gracious and yet haunted, seemed to speak of someone who knew only too well that an uncertain future lay before him. The man was young, perhaps in his early thirties; Sword had children of his own who were similarly aged, though he doubted that any of them were capable of such a completely silent approach.

'Captain Tucker,' Sword addressed the officer, his tone carefully neutral. 'Clearly your regiment have excelled in stealth training. With men like you at Mr Asquith's disposal, the Austrians and Germans won't have a hope of lasting out until Christmas.'

Tucker smiled wanly. 'My apologies, sir. I hadn't realised that you were so deep in thought.'

'Oh, just reminiscing about times gone by. These walls hold a lot of history, you know. Much older than the building; some of it older than Stirling itself.' He gently swept his arm around the room, indicating the ramshackle assembly of crates and boxes. 'It hardly seems credible, when you see it all bundled away like this.'

'My men have taken care of the operation to your satisfaction, I trust?'

Sword grunted. 'Operation? You make it sound like they were fighting the Boers in the gallery, Captain. But to answer your question, yes, they've done a remarkable job in such a short space of time. Thank you.'

'I'm glad,' the officer nodded politely. 'Though they could not have achieved it without your supervision. I did order them to take the utmost care... but time, you will appreciate, is of the essence.'

'You don't need to remind me of that fact, Mr Tucker. I have no more desire to see this place rechristened as the Schmidt Institute than you do.' His grim expression of resolution communicated to the young Captain that this curator was not the type to complain, least of all under the circumstances.

'I'm grateful for your understanding,' Tucker propounded solemnly. 'It has been a difficult time for everyone. But then, we must do as our duty requires.'

'Indeed we must,' Sword agreed with grave sincerity. 'Your responsibility is, as you say, to ensure the defence of the realm... but this building contains the essence of the very culture that you fight to protect. I am thankful that you've given me the time to prepare the collections for storage.'

'I only wish I could've afforded you more, sir. I certainly didn't envy your efforts in having to dismantle the contents of the Institute's museum, to say nothing of the galleries; I trust that you must've been compelled to burn the midnight oil.'

'Yes, well, I did owe the effort to the artists as much as I did to our visitors. People like Thomas Stuart Smith expected their work to be maintained for the decades to come, you know - not rolled up like so much wallpaper.' Sword remembered fondly the first time that he'd seen the watercolour collection that had been painted by Smith, a talented artist who had later become the building's founder. Even after all the intervening years, he could scarcely forget how bright the colours seemed, almost as though they had only been painted the day beforehand. It felt like an eternity ago.

'Probably for the best that he isn't here to see them now,' the curator added resignedly, eyeing the improvised canvas rack. 'I'm willing to wager that he'd be even more upset about it than the Town Clerk has been.'

Tucker arched an eyebrow. 'Mr Buchan Morris, sir?'

'One of our most active Trustees. He loves this place almost as much as my predecessor did,' Sword smiled absently. 'Somehow I doubt either of them would approve of the collection's current accommodation.' This was supposed to be the fortieth anniversary of the Smith's first opening to the public, after all, but regrettably celebration was the furthest thing from anyone's mind for the time being. 'As your colleagues are so fond of saying, however,

10

orders are orders,' he sighed wearily, privately wondering if the galleries would ever be open to the eyes of the community at large again.

Tucker moved further into the makeshift storage area, gazing around the impossibly congested room as he did so. 'If it may be of any consolation, I doubt that they shall be hidden away in here for long. We anticipate that this will be a short and decisive conflict; a few months, perhaps a year at most, and you should be free to return this place to its former glory.'

'I have every trust in your assessment of the situation, Captain,' the curator noted gently, 'but my principal hope for your forecast is that its accuracy will provide a swift and safe return for your regiment.' Sword irritably fingered the rim of his starched collar; his Norfolk jacket had been a poor choice on an afternoon as warm as this, but it had seemed overcast and positively cool earlier in the day thanks to a chill breeze coming in from the Forth.

'We do what we must,' Tucker responded determinedly. 'The honour and security of the Empire is at stake. And as it happens, that's what I wanted to speak with you about.'

Though he had never given voice to the thought, Sword already suspected the true intention of Tucker's visit - and it was far from a mere social call. Why else would the Colonel's right-hand man have come in person at a time like this, rather than sending a subordinate in his place?

11

'The Highlanders will be taking up residence in the Smith Institute from the beginning of next week,' the Captain said smartly, the cadence of his voice brooking no compromise. 'The craft supervisors estimate that the last of their work will be complete within days. Information about the exact battalions which will be situated here is classified, naturally, but we will be taking charge of the building's main door as of now.'

A short, tense pause hung in the air for a moment as the two men regarded each other. The curator was the first to break the silence. 'Well, if nothing else it should mark a welcome change from all this oppressive quiet,' Sword noted introspectively, his face unreadable. 'Whenever the hammering and sawing comes to a halt, I'd swear you could hear a pin drop in here.' In truth, the construction work had been an erratic affair, with carpenters and labourers arriving at all hours only to disappear abruptly when summoned elsewhere in the town. Their constant demands for access to the building at irregular hours had run Sword ragged these past few weeks, and he would be elated when the Institute no longer stank of fresh sawdust.

For the first time, Tucker looked mildly uncomfortable. 'I trust that you received the instructions from the Colonel regarding...'

'My living quarters, yes.' Sword nodded in response. 'I am to have access to this room in order to maintain the collections as necessary, but beyond our private residence neither my family nor myself will have right of entry to any part of the building that is held under military control.' He reeled off the regulation almost as though he had learned it by rote. 'Thank you, Captain. The directives were quite clear.'

The young officer seemed relieved at Sword's ready acceptance of the situation. Clearly, it appeared, this pragmatic custodian of the Institute was a man with whom he could do business. 'The Colonel is looking into the possibility of providing a new doorway to your quarters, sir: perhaps by converting an existing window at the side of the building into a secondary entrance. That should... well, smooth your path somewhat when it comes to separating your day-to-day activities from our own. I would also like to reassure you that I, or a fellow officer, will keep you apprised of any situation that may require your attention. But I would again reiterate that we do not intend to make use of the Institute for any longer than necessity requires.'

Thankful at least to know where the situation now stood, Sword sighed. 'Very well, Mr Tucker. As you can see, I have almost finished my work here. Just a few boxes left to pack, and the Smith will be yours.'

'These remaining items all need to be tagged or numbered, I take it?'

'Every item has already been carefully catalogued at the point of acquisition, Captain - of that fact I can assure you,' Sword said, perhaps more sharply than he'd intended. Did this young man know nothing of curatorship?

'But they were never intended to be packed away with such scant decorum, so I'm simply doing the best I can under the circumstances.'

Tucker nodded abstractedly, his attention focused upon the items arranged on the floor at the curator's feet. 'It appears quite an eclectic assortment that you have there, sir, if I might say.' His eyes swept around to take in a small pile of Roman coins, a selection of bone fragments carefully cushioned upon two layers of tissue paper, something that looked strangely like the detached heel of a gentleman's shoe, and...

'Good Lord,' the officer gasped in ill-disguised awe. 'Is that an emerald?'

Seeming gently amused at the younger man's unabashed astonishment, Sword reached down to the ground as though intending to browse through a small but immaculately organised row of historical objects. Gently brushing aside a few communion tokens and a jagged piece of pottery, he plucked a large green gemstone from the broad stretch of wadding upon which it lay. Scattering jade light onto the floor as it was elevated, the radiant jewel looked to be almost the size of a medium-sized snuff-box. 'An emerald, Mr Tucker? What you see before you is no ordinary cut stone. This, sir, is the Maharajah's Homunculus.'

Tucker's gaze never left the glistening jewel, though the curator strongly suspected that it was the emerald's sheer size rather than its many facets which was entrancing his

14

visitor. 'Would you care to hold it for a moment?' Sword asked the Captain. Somewhat surprised by the suggestion, Tucker nodded his assent with a bob of his head, and Sword carefully placed the gem into the young officer's hand.

Holding the precious stone up to the scarce amount of light that the room's few unexposed windows currently afforded, the Captain squinted slightly as he regarded the gem's delicate contours. 'Extraordinary,' he said after a moment of hushed deliberation. 'Upon my honour, Mr Sword, I've never seen such an intricately presented gemstone in my life. Nor one of such prodigious dimensions.'

'I hadn't taken you for a connoisseur, Captain,' Sword noted tepidly, though not unkindly.

'Oh, you'd be surprised at the sights I've witnessed, sir. When I was stationed at the Khyber Pass, there was no shortage of fine jewellery on display in the courts of the Raj. But by my word, I've never seen anything quite so grand as this.'

'It used to be displayed in this very room once, many years ago,' the curator intoned softly, stroking his greying moustache thoughtfully as he cast his mind back to years long since departed. 'This particular section of the museum was once used specifically to display items of Scottish cultural interest; that was back before it housed the ethnography collection. But - for reasons known only to

15

himself - my predecessor Mr Croall made a temporary exception for this little beauty.'

Gently handing the emerald back to Sword, though with a hesitancy that bordered upon the reluctant, Tucker couldn't help but be intrigued. 'The Maharajah's Homunculus, you called it? A curious name for a precious stone, sir.'

Now finding himself momentarily mesmerised as he turned the gem in his hand, studying its striking patina for the first time in years, Sword's face broke into a nostalgic smile. The green refracted light contained an undeniably hypnotic quality, he could not deny. '"The prince's puppet", Captain, if we're to speak plainly. That might be what it is called, but in truth that emerald always seemed to be the one pulling the strings. All a bit before your own time, if I might say.' The mirth of his expression began to falter. 'It was nothing but trouble back then, and - if I'm to be entirely honest with you - it has the singular honour of being the one item from the Smith's collections that I have no hesitation in packing away out of both sight and mind.'

'But whatever for?' asked Tucker, genuinely surprised as to the cause of the curator's unfathomable dismissiveness. 'Is the emerald under the influence of a curse, sir?'

Sword laughed without humour, his face incredulous. 'Those who coveted it may well have felt as though they were... but on the whole, the stone itself has always seemed like a rather contented wee chap to me.'

'I'm not sure I follow. Are you saying that this stone was once *stolen* from the Institute?'

Though Sword was still looking in the general direction of his guest, the curator's gaze now seemed distant, as though preoccupied with the events of long ago. '"Stolen" can prove to be a very illusive word, Captain. Perhaps "borrowed" would be the more apposite term. But however you choose to look at it, that emerald has a rather chequered history within the Smith, and one that I feel is probably best left to the tender mercies of the passing years.'

Though he fought to keep his expression neutral, Tucker remained fascinated by his host's evasive account. 'Well, if anyone should be well-informed as to the history of this building, Mr Sword, then undeniably it would be you. And if it is your decision that the mystery of this stone should be lost in the mists of time, then so be it.'

'History?' said Sword, his visage appearing ever more inscrutable. 'I'm not warning you about the legacy of this little trinket because I read about it in a dusty book somewhere. No, I'm not warning you because of some old wives' tale.' He stared at Tucker with profound vehemence, the intensity of his eyes growing with every passing word.

'I'm warning you because I was there to see it for myself.'

December 1879

CHAPTER I
An Unexpected Visitor

There was bitterness in the biting winter breeze that prompted the Reverend Sebastian Chappelton to tuck his woollen scarf a little tighter around the neck of his heavy black greatcoat. It seemed to him that there was a dryness to the air here in Scotland that he was altogether unused to; a chill that gnawed into his very bones. The moors back home could be bleak and uncompromising at this time of year, he knew, but somehow the cold felt different this far north, reminding him not for the first time that he was in unfamiliar climes.

The vicar stepped carefully out of the Hansom cab, careful to avoid any icy patches on the pavement beyond, and rummaged in his coat pocket until he had cobbled together enough change to remunerate the driver. The man in the front seat had a ruddy, jovial appearance, looking considerably more patient than his poor horse in the harsh winter cold, and thanked the clergyman with gusto as the coins were pressed firmly into his hand. Noticing the generous tip which had been included with his payment, the driver thanked Chappelton with frosted breath and wished him a heartfelt 'Merry Christmas' before snapping his reins, his equine companion cantering off along Dumbarton Road as it pulled the cab off towards the King's Park.

Now alone on the street, Chappelton turned to regard his surroundings. He was a tall, gangly man with a pale, almost pasty complexion, his habitually creased brow and horn-rimmed spectacles lending him a professorial air which perpetually made him appear older than his forty years. Squinting through his eyeglasses against the low, watery winter sun, the vicar took a moment to orient himself in his new location. Set high upon a towering rocky ledge was the commanding sight of Stirling Castle, its instantly recognisable position from all areas of the town suggesting that the medieval stronghold was even now keeping watch over its ancient domain. Yet at ground level, even taking into account a small row of residential town-houses across the street, there was only one building which dominated this end of the road; a grand and solidly-built structure with an appealing Greco-Roman facade, its presence amongst the nearby grassy parkland and marshy ground made it appear at once both inviting and enigmatic. The sheer dimensions of the architecture made it unmistakeable even from quite some distance, the large windows seeming efficiently spaced amongst the grand blocks of light sandstone. It had been a harsh winter thus far, and the vestiges of a recent hard frost could be seen glistening in various places along the outer surface of the masonry. There was even a hint of snow scattered here and there amongst the expansive, verdant grounds, not least upon the spikes of the wrought-iron railings which encircled their perimeter.

Hugging his coat closer to himself, the vicar wandered along the paved walkway towards the large building's main doors, his pace slow enough to allow him time to drink in the details of its exterior. The imposing Doric portico - four grand pillars framing the main doorway - was crowned by a large sandstone tympanum, bearing a prominent family coat of arms (presumably that of the building's founder) which was bordered by the famous Stirling Wolf on one side and the Castle on the other. Directly above the doorway was an inscription, 'THE SMITH INSTITUTE', in large lettering; beneath it upon the entablature could be read the words 'Erected and endowed with funds bequeathed by Thomas Stuart Smith of Glassingall Perthshire'. There was, the cold-rife cleric assured himself wryly, little danger that he had arrived at the wrong address.

A solitary robin was singing in the grounds, its tunefulness diminishing in Chappelton's wake as he stepped through the main doorway into an entry vestibule. The vicar narrowed his eyes momentarily as they adjusted to the Institute's interior. Though it was by no means dark inside the building, passing out of the bright winter sunlight briefly made it appear so. The familiar smoky smell of coal and wood expelled from household chimneys along the street faded away as he passed into the high-ceilinged entrance antechamber. Directly in front of him was a grand revolving doorway in gleaming mahogany and glass.

Pushing against one of its immaculately polished brass handles, the clergyman soon found himself in much warmer surroundings as he swept through into the Smith's foyer. The hallway was long, decorated in neutral colours with broad flagstones forming the floor. A number of oil lamps were fitted along the wall on either side, though at this time of day none of them had yet been ignited. All of these incidental details, however, seemed inconsequential given the room's unmistakeably seasonal focal point. A huge pine tree stood at the top of a small flight of stairs, its broad trunk dominating the area. Each of its branches had been carefully decorated with squat white candles, a broad skirt arranged around the base of its trunk in order to catch the wax as it fell. From his initial glance, it was obvious to Chappelton that none of the candles had yet been lit, their untrimmed wicks and uniform length suggesting that the tree was a relatively new arrival in the Institute.

'It's a braw thing, sir, is it no'?' came a strong, deep voice with a broad accent native to the area. Caught momentarily unaware, Chappelton span around on his heel to face a squat man, perhaps in his mid-fifties, with thinning silver hair and a buoyant, laughing

24

face. He was attired in warm if somewhat utilitarian tweed clothing, his woollen fingerless gloves suggesting that he too had been feeling the cold recently. Noticing the newcomer's startled expression, the smaller man immediately struck a conciliatory tone as he emerged from the shadow of the doorway. 'I'm awfy sorry if I surprised ye there. It wisnae intended, I can assure ye.'

'No need to apologise,' the vicar smiled thinly. His voice was quiet, almost subdued, though it managed to carry through the still air regardless. 'I was just admiring your festive decorations. And by the look of things, there's certainly no small amount to appreciate.'

The man with the gloves nodded enthusiastically. 'That's very true, sir. Aye, true indeed. It only arrived late on last night, all the way from Kippen. It's a wee village up the road there, and... well, would ye credit it, they thought they could get it through the revolving door. Can ye imagine?' He chuckled to himself at the very thought. 'We had to bring it in and roun' through the reading room instead.' He indicated towards a broad doorway in the entrance vestibule, adjacent to the main door, and then kept pointing as his finger coasted towards another door further along the hallway. 'As it happens, I didnae get around to sprucing it up until this morning. The curator, ye see; he insisted it's bad luck to put up decorations before Christmas Eve. Which is a strange thing, in a way,' he added conspiratorially, 'because he's no' by any means a superstitious man.'

Impressed by his host's fastidiousness, Chappelton's forehead furrowed in surprise. 'Well, if you've managed such a feat in just a couple of hours then I feel you're to be congratulated, Mr...?'

'McLafferty, sir. Jimmy McLafferty. I'm the museum assistant.' The vicar covertly noted the way that the diminutive man was tacitly sizing him up, as though suspicious of his unfamiliar accent. 'Might I take yer coat, please?'

'You're very kind,' Chappelton smiled. He gently shrugged his way out of his long dark outer-garment, unfurling his scarf before handing both to McLafferty. Upon seeing the stark white strip of the visitor's dog collar exposed when he had removed his coat, the assistant nodded respectfully.

'Yer a man of the cloth, sir?' he asked guardedly, his curiosity no less piqued by the stranger's enunciation - an educated mode of inflection which, with its mix of neutral intonation and occasional regional nuances, may have originated anywhere from Yorkshire to the Midlands. 'Forgive me for sayin' so, but ye sound to me as though yer no' fae round these parts.'

Chappelton nodded in agreement. 'Then your assumption is quite correct. I am but a visitor here in Stirling... and pleased to be so, if I may add.'

McLafferty inclined his head in response, too polite to enquire further. Instead, folding the vicar's coat carefully over his arm, he said: 'If ye've come to see the paintings, I'm afraid ye've left yerself little time, sir. The light's going already, and if ye had a mind to see them tae full advantage...'

'Thank you, Mr McLafferty,' the visitor responded crisply. 'I do realise that one must take account of the early nightfall this far north.' It was not so very long past the Shortest Day, after all, and with winter appearing to have set in early the skies had seemed permanently overcast ever since he had arrived in the town. 'But as it happens, I have not come to view your Institute's paintings - splendid though I have no doubt they are,' he added hastily, keen not to offend.

'The reading room, then?' asked McLafferty, clearly eager to show his guest all customary hospitality. 'We have nae shortage of lamps in there, sir, so ye neednae be held hostage tae the sunlight the way ye'd be in the galleries. There's also the distinct advantage of a fine roaring coal fire, which I'm sure any gentleman would find most invitin' on an afternoon such as this.'

The good-humoured attendant started off along the hallway, seeming keen to usher the visitor into warmer and more inviting surroundings. Taking a few steps down the foyer, he neared a beautiful grandfather clock in the modern design which, though ticking stridently with scrupulous precision, seemed

27

dwarfed by the scale of its newly-arrived evergreen neighbour. Although Chappelton followed at a respectful distance, more than willing to put additional space between himself and the draught of the main doorway, he cleared his throat politely as they neared the intended destination. 'Appealing though the prospect of a warm hearth and the perusal of today's papers may seem, Mr McLafferty, I'm afraid that was not the intention of my visit either. Though I do thank you for the kind thought nonetheless.'

Seeming surprised at the cleric's ambiguous statement, the museum assistant cocked his head quizzically. 'Then how might I be of assistance tae ye, sir?'

'There is one overarching reason for my presence here today, and it is that I have come to visit the curator of this Institute: the eminent Mr Alexander Croall.'

Bemused, McLafferty seemed slightly chastened by this announcement. 'Forgive me, Minister. I hadnae realised you were here on business. Or, for that matter, that yer business was wi' Mr Croall.'

Chappelton grinned disarmingly. 'It's "Vicar", actually. And I assure you that there is no need for apology either; the objective of my call is not an occupational one, strictly speaking, but simply to convey the compliments of the season.'

'Um... aye,' said the increasingly puzzled attendant. 'Well, if ye'd be so kind as to follow me, sir, I'll be more than glad to take ye up to the curator. I've nae doubt he'll be delighted to receive ye; things are usually fair quiet here on Christmas Eve, ye know.' With impeccable cordiality, he added by way of an afterthought: 'Mr Croall is always grateful of a guest to entertain.'

Wasting no time, McLafferty swept away from the doorway and the rhythmic tick of the clock. The aroma of pine needles grew stronger as he brushed by the tree and moved up a small flight of steps, passing a fine oil painting of a bearded man with piercing, knowledgeable eyes. Though the figure's thinning hair had begun to turn grey at the time of his portraiture, his wise face had retained more than a hint of youthful vigour. Chappelton couldn't help but pause momentarily to regard this sagacious character who stared out at him, the figure's gaze both worldly and strangely questioning. The vicar had only stopped his motion for a matter of seconds, but already his nimble host was striding into the gallery beyond. For such a sturdy, compact man, McLafferty was surprisingly light on his feet.

Smartly picking up his pace, the visitor followed past the Christmas tree through the bulky double-doors leading from the hallway into the gallery... and immediately found himself looking around in astonishment at the sight which met him there. Top-lit from an intricate glass skylight, the dying afternoon sun bathed the room in soft crepuscular hues, illuminating four walls of deep maroon which

29

were covered from ceiling to floor with neatly-framed watercolour paintings. 'Remarkable,' he muttered under his breath. 'Quite extraordinary.' Though Chappelton had visited other galleries over the years, he was the first to admit that he was no aficionado, and he had never seen quite so many works of art clustered together as was the case here. The paintings stretched from below eye level all the way up to the room's soft green coving and, although rural panoramas and marine vistas appeared to predominate in many places, the subject of each painting seemed completely different from every one which had come before it.

'An impressive sight, sir, I'm sure ye'll agree,' opined McLafferty, who slowed his movement slightly without being in any danger of nearing a standstill. 'Most of what ye see here was painted by the building's founder, the late Mr Thomas Stuart Smith. Ye may have seen his portrait out in the foyer over yonder.'

So that had been the identity of that curiously Orphic figure by the clock: the shrewd-looking yet seemingly pensive man in the oil painting who had been staring austerely out at the Institute's new Christmas tree. No wonder his expression had been so enquiring; from the portrait's vantage point it was almost as though Smith himself was able to mutely assess each and every visitor to his Institute, passing unspoken judgement upon them as they passed into the gallery to view his works. 'He certainly appears to have been prolific in his day,' Chappelton said, his voice betraying no small amount of admiration.

'That he was, sir. That he was.' The vicar couldn't help but distinguish a note of wistfulness in McLafferty's voice as he added: 'Mr Smith was but a young man when he passed, many would say before his time, and 'twas a tragedy that he never lived to see the foundations of this place dug intae the ground. But still, may he rest in peace knowing that the fruits of his craft survived him.'

Although the parson felt slightly cheated at having to sweep through the gallery without expending any amount of time viewing the artworks on display, even in the dimming light, he noticed that his acquaintance's countenance seemed to brighten again as they passed through another large double doorway. McLafferty beamed as he regarded the contents of the cavernous room which lay beyond, as though he saw it for the first time each and every time that he entered. For Chappelton, whose eyes were indeed comprehending its contours anew, the sight was undeniably impressive. The exhibition space beyond was enormous, easily three or four times the size of the previous gallery, and its walls were bedecked - seemingly covering just about every free inch of space - by framed paintings as far as the eye could see. The room shared its predecessor's maroon and green colour scheme, but the high vaulted glass ceiling here was much larger, allowing considerably more light into the gallery even in spite of the relentless encroachment of dusk. Whereas the lower gallery had exclusively contained watercolour paintings, however, this exhibition space seemed to have been reserved for oils and fine art of all kinds; portraits and landscapes alike could be seen in various places, alongside still-life scenes and pictographic representations of ancient mythology. The juxtaposition was highly arresting, and the carefully-considered positioning of each painting added to the room's general sense of both grandeur and airiness.

McLafferty was weaving his way along the middle of the room, marching past a line of wooden benches designed for public seating which had been spaced evenly throughout both sides of the gallery. 'Were ye to ask me, sir, I'd tell ye that this is the pride of the Smith Institute. A' human life is up on thae walls for a'body to see. I've worked here since the place opened, ye ken, and still yet I can find myself looking at something in here that I've never clapped eyes on before.'

Following the sure-footed assistant along the gallery, acutely aware of the fact that he had no time even to register the paintings that he was passing, Chappelton courteously enquired: 'You are indeed most accommodating, Mr McLafferty.'

'Aye, well, it's good of ye to say so, Reverend,' the attendant replied with a modest inclination of his head. 'We dae like our guests to feel welcome.'

'So, if I might ask... are you the head of the Institute's front of house staff?'

'No, sir,' he replied, seeming barely able to stifle a polite laugh. 'I *am* the Institute's front of house staff.'

'Then you are to be doubly commended, I feel,' the vicar pronounced earnestly as they finally neared the far end of the vast gallery. He could not help but feel that his companion had purposely brought him via the scenic route. 'It is greatly to your credit that such palpable care and attention is lavished upon a public area to this extent.'

'Thank ye, Minist... I mean, Vicar,' said McLafferty, inclining his head in respect of the compliment. 'When I'm sweeping the floors and polishing the door-handles at six of a mornin', it's gratifying tae ken that *somebody* notices.' With practiced grace, he headed for another large doorway which was situated in an internal wall adjacent to the rear of the gallery. 'If ye'll follow me through here, please.'

The next area seemed even longer than the main gallery, though not quite as broad. This, Chappelton felt sure, must be the Smith's main museum. Even better stocked than he'd been led to believe, it was immediately clear that it held a veritable cornucopia of artefacts spanning the centuries – and not all of them originating in Stirling itself, it seemed. A number of large windows allowed light in to illuminate the exhibits and, given their situation on the east side of the building, they took full advantage of the dying sunlight to cast warm orange luminosity over the many display cases lining the room; an inviting radiance that seemed to belie the stark winter frost outside. Those wooden and glass cases were carefully placed around all four of the museum's walls, in an evident attempt to fill as much of the spacious area as possible with the artefacts which were available for public view. The room's decor seemed blander than that of the galleries somehow, its grey and beige livery suggesting that the decorators had been instructed not to allow the colour scheme to distract the attention of visitors from the panoply of exhibits on display. And what a feast for the eyes they were; social history and natural history rubbed shoulders throughout the room, with archaeological objects of interest such as ancient coinage and stone axe-heads displayed in one area of the room, only to be bordered by pieces of pottery on one side and communion tokens on the other. Along the centre of the room were glass-topped display tables, each of them bearing a very different range of smaller items which complimented well the grander exhibits showcased in the surrounding cabinets.

Yet for all the varied artefacts competing for his attention, Chappelton found himself immediately focusing instead upon the centre of the room. There, busying himself with a large, currently open display case, was a man in late middle age - with his sprightly movements, one would be loath to consider him yet elderly - dressed all in black, the only hint of any lighter shade being the white cravat protruding from the neck of his frock coat. The garment appeared to have seen better days, with various rags and dusters overhanging from its capacious pockets. Yet to all appearances the coat seemed to double as something of a curatorial toolbox, the chalk-marks on its sleeves and light dust upon its tails speaking of many unseen travails in the course of its owner's duties. Glass bottles, presumably containing preservative agents and other chemicals, were arranged carefully around the base of the large man-sized wooden box where the industrious gentleman was presently standing. As the vicar was led closer by McLafferty to the older man's position, Chappelton could see a shock of snowy hair and a pair of great white whiskers framing his face, tapering down to a full beard. Though his features were wrinkled now, the gentleman had somehow managed to retain an air of careworn youthfulness. When he turned to regard the source of the approaching footsteps, Chappelton found the man's eyes to be warm and - in their twinkling curiosity - almost bordering on the mischievous.

'Mr McLafferty,' the eccentric-looking gentleman said, his tenor curious but not unwelcoming. 'I cannot fail to observe that you have brought a visitor with you.' Though his deep voice carried an intonation that was largely redolent of the Scottish Highlands, in its gentrification Chappelton had difficulty placing his accent more precisely. The man in

35

black straightened himself up, wiping his hands on a rag plucked from his pocket which was just as swiftly returned. 'At this hour a cup of tea would have been almost as welcome, but a guest - well, that is something to be celebrated, I'm sure.'

As the vicar moved nearer to regard the man at a respectful distance, a faint but unmistakably pungent chemical aroma in the air as his proximity increased, he was finally in a position to see the item that was currently being worked on inside the case. A strange set of armour was arranged upon a featureless wooden mannequin, the likes of which he had never before cast his eyes upon. Its construction seemed entirely foreign to him, and certainly did not seem British - indeed, not even European. Sensing his visitor's bewilderment, the bearded man elucidated: 'A recent addition to the Institute's collections - eighteenth century, I believe, from the Japanese *Edo* period. *Samurai*, you know. You'll note the design of the *kusari katabira* - the chain armour jacket - and the *hachi-gane* forehead protection, which dates it to the last century. I think I'm correct in my conjecture, Mr McLafferty - wouldn't you?'

'Aye, very probably, Mr Croall,' replied the assistant cheerfully, his puzzled expression revealing his true feelings on the matter. 'In fact, I'd concur with ye wholeheartedly.'

'Splendid!' he grinned, clapping his hands together with enthusiasm. 'A fascinating piece, as you can see, but getting a shine on all of those little iron *tetsu* scales is a job unto itself, let me tell you.' Before the thunderstruck Chappelton had an opportunity to respond, the man immediately supplemented his account with: 'Welcome to the Smith Institute, by the way.' He extended his hand, and in spite of the man's advancing years Chappelton found the grip of his shake to be both firm and sincere as he reciprocated in kind.

'Your welcome is greatly appreciated, sir.' The mystified clergyman blinked hard, somewhat bemused by his host's eccentric manner. 'But if I might ask, do I have the pleasure of addressing Mr Alexander Croall?'

'Your humble servant, Reverend.' He inclined his head courteously. 'I am the curator of this building, and glad to be at your disposal.'

'Then I count myself privileged to have shaken the hand which composed *The Nature Printed British Seaweeds*. A remarkable work, sir - all four volumes of it.'

'Good gracious me!' Croall exclaimed, clearly delighted at the recognition. 'You flatter me, Reverend, in remembering such a dusty tome from twenty years back.'

Chappelton found his host's self-effacing humility to be above reproach, knowing too well that the influential book was far from a vague scholarly volume. 'You are far too modest, sir. The standard work on any subject can hardly be considered a mere trifle.'

'Standard work, you say, eh?' The curator smiled dryly. 'Why, I spent so long researching it, my colleagues began calling me "Roosty Tangle". And at any rate, the same hand that put pen to paper on that scientific manuscript was just this very morning hard at work preserving a human skull - another new acquisition, you know - so I do hope that I remembered to wash it afterwards.'

Before Chappelton had the opportunity to enquire further about Croall's abstruse statement, a large door at the opposite end of the museum burst open, admitting what seemed to be a small typhoon into the room. As his gaze adjusted to the fast-approaching tumult the vicar noted that the flurry of activity came not from any climatic phenomena, but rather from a young boy who was even now racing towards their position. He was smartly dressed, presumably hailing from a comfortable background judging by the cut of his clothes, though his dark hair was wild and matted - no doubt from some unseen outdoor adventure. He looked to be perhaps eleven or twelve years of age.

'Mr Croall!' the boy cried as he tore towards the curator... and then slowed his pace as he realised that the older man was currently entertaining an as-yet-unknown visitor. 'I'm sorry, Mr Croall,' he mumbled by way of apology. 'I didn't realise you were expecting guests.'

'How many times have I to tell ye, laddie?' McLafferty barked. 'No running in the Institute!' Although his inflection was sharp, he could not disguise his obvious fondness for the earnest-looking young man.

'It's alright, Davie,' the dusty custodian smiled indulgently. 'You weren't to know. Ah! But introductions are called for. Sir,' he added, turning around to address Chappelton, 'may I introduce David Buchan Morris - the finest young assistant any curator could ask for.'

'A pleasure I'm sure, Master Buchan Morris,' the vicar nodded solemnly at the tousled youngster. The exuberance of the youth of today!

Davie rummaged around in one of the voluminous pockets of his jacket, dislodging a home-made catapult and at least two pieces of string before triumphantly producing a small glass bottle. He handed it to Croall gingerly, as though it were an ingot of solid gold. 'There you are, Mr Croall. The pharmacist said that he'd made it up for you from the instructions you gave him, just like you'd asked.'

'Thank you, Davie,' Croall said with a sly grin as he considered the handwritten scrawl on the bottle's label. 'This will be most helpful.'

Davie then rifled through another pocket for a moment before producing a few copper coins. 'Here's the change too, sir,' he said, handing them over. 'They did say at the chemists' that if you had any other orders, they'd gladly attend to them.'

'Did they, indeed? Well, that's very magnanimous of them.' The curator considered the coins for a moment, then kept one separate from the others and handed it back to the boy. 'That's for your trouble, Davie.'

The young lad's eyes widened as he regarded the coin. 'Really, sir? That's awfy kind of you, Mr Croall.'

'"Awfully", Davie. "Awfully kind." And... well, you deserve it, what with it being Christmas Eve, after all.' He turned to the vicar, affording him a theatrical wink. 'You see, Reverend? That's professional dedication for you. Now, Davie, you be a good lad and go with Mr McLafferty; no doubt he'll need a hand closing up soon.'

'A hand?' Adopting his best drill sergeant's pose, McLafferty fixed the boy with a fearsome stare. 'Aye, a hand aff the back of yer heid's what you want, Davie. You come with me now and leave pair Mr Croall here in peace.'

The young man excused himself politely, and the peculiar couple strolled off towards the galleries, McLafferty closing the door smartly behind them. 'It seems that your curatorial staff commence their duties at a young age in Stirling, sir,' Chappelton noted drolly. 'If I only had half his energy.'

'Davie is a good lad,' Croall smiled. 'He loves this place dearly. Indeed, he has been our most regular guest ever since the doors first opened five years ago.'

'He must be devoted to the Institute indeed, to be out running errands for you this close to Christmas - a time when most children have other pursuits in mind.'

The curator nodded sagely. 'Well, my health is not what it once was. Davie is kind enough to help me in my endeavours from time to time.'

'And don't his family come looking for him?' Chappelton asked, politely confused.

'Oh, they did at first. But now they know exactly where he shall be if they ever need to find him. He is fortunate to have two loving parents, if I'm honest with you. Not all of the children in Stirling are so fortunate. If you were to ask my daughter Annie about some of the sights she's seen...' Trailing off, seemingly self-conscious at his unintended reverie, Croall quickly decided to change the subject. 'Anyway, Davie will always be more than welcome here as long as he wishes to visit; if my time as a schoolmaster back in Montrose taught me anything, it is that an enquiring mind is something that should be nourished and never discouraged.'

The vicar frowned curiously. 'You were a schoolteacher, Mr Croall?' It appeared that his host was clearly a polymath indeed.

'A joiner too at one point, to say nothing of an amateur archaeologist in my day,' the curator laughed amiably. 'I am not sure which was the more tiring job, truth to tell, though both experiences have come in useful since I started work here at the Institute.' He held up the bottle that Davie had handed him, squinting through the glass as he regarded the gelatinous liquid suspension held within. 'Yes, this should do nicely.'

41

'A medication from your pharmacist, might I presume?'

Croall shook his head, never taking his eyes off the bottle as he again checked the contents of the label. 'Only in a manner of speaking, sir. This is preservative agent... and, in a way, a kind of polish to aid in the augmentation of the patina. It is a compound fashioned to my specifications, after some correspondence with a chemist friend of mine, in the hope that it will help to maintain a particular item beyond its natural lifespan.'

'The skull that you mentioned earlier, perhaps?' The vicar's countenance now appeared thoroughly perplexed. 'A human skull, you said? Whyever should such an item have a place in your Institute's collections, sir?'

'Well, we must do something to act as a warning against those patrons who refuse to pay the admission fee, mustn't we?' Croall chuckled quietly to himself, though - keen not to risk offending his guest - he hastily added: 'The exhibit of which I speak is no mere fragment of bone and enamel, Reverend. It is a replica cast from our late monarch, His Highness King Robert the Bruce... and not simply a reproduction of the famous William Scoular plaster cast, at that. Therefore, choosing the right substance to prepare it will be of paramount importance - one would of course baulk at using a wood polish to add lustre to metalwork, for instance.'

'Quite so,' agreed Chappelton, wondering what material the replica actually *had* been cast from. His host appeared to be running some way ahead of trend in his use of such techniques.

'Time is of the essence, you see. Soon the exhibit will be joining the Scottish history collection that is taking form in the Institute's lower museum, so that it may be viewed by any who choose to visit.' The curator paused ruminatively for a moment before continuing. 'I trust, though, that natural history must be of greater interest to you, given your earlier familiarity with my work.'

'Would that that were true, sir. I am but a humble man of God, with little understanding of such issues. My knowledge of your text, which I am honoured to say I have viewed in all its splendour, derives from my acquaintance with a certain colleague in the clergy whom I believe may be all too well known to you: the Reverend William Croall.'

Croall blinked, the revelation seeming to catch him off-guard. 'William? My word, sir! You're a friend of my son, then?'

'My parish is in Whinmoor, not so very far from William's church in Leeds. And yes, we have come to build a friendship these past few years. I have greatly valued his opinion on many matters, whether personal or spiritual.'

'Indeed, my boy always made acquaintances easily. A listening ear is a good ear, as the old adage goes. Though I suspect that these virtues are a gift better attributed to his mother than myself.' The skin around Croall's eyes wrinkled as his face broke into a wide grin.

'Perhaps your son has made mention of me in his correspondence?' Chappelton ventured enquiringly.

'William speaks of many people in his letters,' came the tactful reply. 'But of course, it goes without saying that any friend of his is naturally a friend of my own. However - and I do hope that you will forgive me - I don't believe I caught your name?'

The vicar seemed momentarily aghast. 'My dear sir, I do beg your pardon. My lack of propriety shames me. The Reverend Sebastian Chappelton, at your service. And I seek nothing more than to wish you and your family the compliments of the festive season, a sentiment shared both by your son and myself. I assure you that he would sooner have joined me here than not, but professional duties detain him.'

'As I mentioned earlier, Mr Chappelton, you are more than welcome here at the Smith Institute, and I hope that you enjoy your stay. Young William's absence is one which has left a gap in the lives of my wife and myself, to say nothing of those of his sisters, so I am especially grateful to hear news of him. After all, if he believes that his vocational calling is from Almighty God then what kind of father would I be to argue with his convictions?'

'It gives me great pleasure then, sir, to assure you that your son is in good health, and very much at home in his work. He has become a popular figure both with his congregation and indeed with the parish at large. Great things are expected of him, I think it fair to observe.'

'That is kind of you to say. He writes whenever time allows him, as it happens... though rarely at this time of year, given the pressures of Christmas which inevitably come to bear upon any clergyman's schedule. A season of peace and goodwill for all except those who must write the sermons and visit the home of each in his flock - I trust I speak truthfully, Vicar?'

'Quite so,' Chappelton smiled thinly, his voice suddenly soft. 'Though for myself, this will be the first Christmas in nearly two decades where I shall be free of such pressures.'

The curator inclined his head, his expression more concerned than inquisitive. 'You have made alternative arrangements at your parish, perhaps? Surely after twenty years, even the hardest-working cleric deserves some degree of respite.'

'It is... not quite as easily explained as that, sir.' Chappelton could hear his own voice cracking. His expression seemed to betray an inward loathing, as though he was breaking a promise to himself that he would retain his composure. 'The situation was as unexpected to me as my presence has been to you.'

No stranger to empathy, Croall clapped Chappelton on the shoulder, his grip gentle but firm. 'Perhaps it is a matter best discussed in private, sir. For someone who has travelled such a great distance, a little Scotch hospitality is the very least that I can offer.'

* * *

'And so they buried her only two weeks ago. The Bishop himself conducted the service, may God bless him. But even as they lowered her into the ground, I simply couldn't believe what I was seeing. She was three years younger than me, sir; only in her late thirties. And yet there was nothing I could do for her. Nothing!'

'Consumption is a most pitiless enemy, sir; a scourge upon the world,' Croall murmured as he poured a measure of rich red port from a decanter into a crystal glass. 'It has no predisposition upon whom it should claim, whether it be the upper echelons of royalty or a devoted young person such as your late wife. Please be assured that you have my condolences, and those of my family.'

Croall and Chappelton were seated in the curator's private office, a comfortably-sized room situated just next to the Institute's main entrance. The building's administrative centre bore many resemblances to its owner; though seemingly chaotic on the surface, the large oak-panelled desk strewn with various papers and a letter-spike crammed with various correspondence from all over the globe, there were signs too of careful organisation and eclectic tastes. A huge map of the Earth was spread over the far wall behind Croall's desk, the territories of the British Empire shaded in deep pink hues. There was also a complex-looking filing system in evidence, which looked to Chappelton as though its contents had been rescued from the aftermath of a tsunami, though he did not doubt for a moment that every one of its records had been completed with painstaking accuracy. The only thing in the office that seemed even to be even reasonably approaching tidiness was a small pewter desk set - which Croall assured him had been a gift from his three daughters - that held an elaborate collection of pens and an ink-pot along with an ample supply of sealing wax.

Croall carefully laid the decanter down onto a nearby occasional table; the port within sloshed gently as the vessel came to rest on the surface. The companionable silence which had existed between them now began to grow slightly uncomfortable as the curator lowered himself back into his chair, staring wordlessly across his cluttered desk at the reticent visitor. Chappelton, for his part, found himself staring out of the office's window, which offered a commanding view of the front of the building - its hedges, trees and railings - through the frame of its Greco-Roman portico.

'I trust that Stirling will be enjoying the pleasure of your company for a while then, sir?' Croall asked with emphatic geniality, though it seemed to Chappelton that the curator's eyes were watching closely for the manner of his response.

'Of that, I am as yet unsure. My sabbatical is finite, as well you might imagine, for my duty is to my flock.' He looked up, rather more brusquely than intended, to meet Croall's gaze. 'I will not forget my Archdeacon's kindness in allowing me this period of respite. I have always so desired to see the Scotland that William has mentioned so fondly. In this time of mourning and contemplation... it seemed fitting, somehow.'

Croall smiled wanly. 'And you are most welcome here, Reverend, as I said. In your pilgrimage you follow in a proud tradition that includes within it Stuart monarchs and - in more recent years - many admirers of Sir Walter Scott. No doubt William himself would have desired to see more of Scotland than has been the case in recent years; at least when I worked at Derby Museum, the distance between us would never have seemed so insurmountable.' Clearing his throat, he broke through the haze of wistfulness. 'You are staying locally, might I presume?'

'Yes indeed,' Chappelton nodded readily, taking another gentle sip of his port. 'At the Waverley Temperance Hotel.'

'In Murray Place, yes. A fine establishment.'

'You know it, then?'

'Guests of mine have stayed there while visiting Stirling over the years. I am told that their hospitality is impeccable.'

The vicar agreed eagerly. 'Just as yours has been, sir. And yet I must ask you to forgive me, for I feel as though I've neglected your Institute's collections almost entirely.'

Croall held his hand up in a placatory gesture. 'No apology is necessary, sir - I assure you that entertaining your company has been the greatest of pleasures.' Bringing his hand back down onto his desk, he inadvertently ruffled a pile of papers and - noticing one particular letter of note - idly cast an eye over it before declaring: 'Blast! That dispatch from Mr Darwin. I really have been remiss in my response.'

'Mr *Charles* Darwin, sir?' asked Chappelton, his eyes widening.

'None other.' The vicar couldn't disabuse himself of the notion that Croall was fighting against an expression of mirth as he reached for the top drawer of his desk and plucked out a small clay pipe. 'A very welcome correspondent of mine over the years when it comes to botanical matters,' he added, 'though one would not need to be an Archbishop to know that his findings have provoked no small degree of controversy these past two decades.'

'You have a gift for understatement, Mr Croall,' Chappelton spluttered as the curator began stuffing his pipe with tobacco. 'Your acquaintance has provoked no end of debate, regardless of whether one's interest is scientific or theological.'

Croall grinned disarmingly, though his guest knew without question that his response was still being watched intently. With his wily, birdlike movements, the curator looked to Chappelton like a wise old owl sizing up a particularly promising rodent, his congenial demeanour never quite disguising the incisiveness of his observation. 'Yet surely debate is never a bad thing, Reverend - regardless of someone's calling.' Striking a match, he added: 'After all, if we are to believe that the Lord God created the human race, was he not indirectly responsible for the creation of our sciences too?'

'Had the Holy Father intended a species of unthinking automata, sir, He could just as easily have created one,' the vicar responded carefully. 'But there exists a fine line between epistemological conjecture and blasphemy. It is, to say the least, very much a matter of opinion.'

'Excellent!' exclaimed the curator, tapping his desk briskly in agreement as he took an abundant puff of his now-lit pipe. 'An enquiring mind! Something just as much to be valued in a theologian as in a scientist. After all, it is surely no less important to ask *why* as it is to ask *how*.' He paused meditatively for a moment before venturing: 'You did mention that you may be staying in town for a while. Might I enquire as to whether you have any plans for the evening of Saturday the 27th?'

The question seemed to catch Chappelton off guard. 'That would be this very weekend, sir?' Considering the issue momentarily, he shook his head. 'I have no plans. At least, none that come immediately to mind.'

'In that case, Reverend, I would very much like to extend you an invitation - and as you are a guest in our fine town, it is a matter of sincere gratification to do so.' Blowing another wisp of smoke from his pipe, he peered at Chappelton over the cluttered paperwork and assembled paraphernalia on his desk. 'On Saturday, the Smith Institute will be holding a special event in commemoration of the tenth year following the death of its late founder, Mr Thomas Stuart Smith. A celebration of his life's work, if you will - to say nothing of the lasting effects of his bequest, given that it also marks five years since the galleries and museum first opened to the public.'

'Gracious me,' the vicar said wonderingly. 'This is an unexpected honour, Mr Croall. I must confess that I am not entirely sure what to say.'

'Well, if you should be asking my advice, I would warmly recommend saying yes,' the Institute's custodian smiled kindly. 'There will be an exhibition of fine art on display... and, to mark the occasion, I also have something rather special planned.' He made the latter pronouncement with no small amount of pride, though the young clergyman felt certain that his host would offer nothing further on the issue so as to avoid spoiling the surprise. 'If you seek to know more about Stirling, you could ask for no better introduction. Some of the finest talents in the town will be in attendance here on the 27th, and it would give me no greater pleasure than to present you into their company.'

Placing his glass of port on the desk before him, Chappelton rose to his feet and - for the second time that day - extended his hand to his host. 'How could I consider any course of action other than to accept your kind offer, sir - and with the greatest of satisfaction, what is more. Your hospitality has been generous almost beyond words.'

Standing to accept his guest's outreached hand, Croall seemed genuinely delighted that his proposal had been met with such wholehearted consent. 'Marvellous, sir. Yes, quite so. And, if I may offer my personal assurance,' he added with a characteristic twinkle in his eye, 'the Smith Institute will undoubtedly promise you an evening to remember.'

CHAPTER II
Many Arrivals

It seemed to the Reverend Chappelton that Mr Croall's guarantee had been realised within mere moments of his arrival at the Smith Institute on the evening of that final Saturday in December. He was to enter the main foyer, glad of shelter from the icy cold of the night, to discover that the building had undergone a veritable transformation since the time of his previous visit a mere handful of days beforehand.

The first and most apparent change - quite apart from the hallway's wall-mounted oil lamps each having been ignited, casting the room in a warm and inviting glow - was the fact that the Institute's expansive pine tree was now nothing less than a blaze of light, its many candles carefully lit and glimmering like dozens of individual little stars dancing on the end of each branch. The festive jollity on display helped in some small part to distract Chappelton from the melancholy of his own, solitary Christmas, overly conscious of his introverted status while (he was all too acutely aware) families around him celebrated the season in their own way. Life goes on, as the old saying went, and the vicar could not in good conscience begrudge others from enjoying one brief bright spot in what promised to be a long and unforgiving winter.

The contrast to his earlier call at the Smith could not be more pronounced, for whereas the timing of his prior visit had seen the galleries largely empty of visitors he imagined that its current status had far more in common with its everyday operation; dozens of smartly-dressed guests mingled convivially from room to room, wishing each other the compliments of the season with heartfelt sincerity. Suddenly feeling somewhat self-conscious at his lack of a partner for the evening, the vicar moved a few steps in from the building's revolving door when he heard someone familiar clearing their throat nearby.

'Good evening tae ye, Mr Chappelton,' piped up the perennially jovial Jimmy McLafferty. He was certainly clad in his Sunday best this evening, a neatly pressed suit and crisply-presented cravat complementing a smart pair of shoes which looked as though they had received an entire month's supply of spit and polish. 'It's good that ye were able to join us.'

'I wouldn't have missed it for the world, Mr McLafferty,' replied Chappelton, diligently handing over his coat before the conscientious assistant felt the need to ask. There had been fresh snowfall outside and the wind had grown ever more bitterly cold these past few days, so he was especially relieved to discover that the Institute's interior was appealingly temperate. 'If your enchanting decorations were not enough, it is certainly nothing less than a delight to be in the warm on a night like this.'

McLafferty nodded in heartfelt agreement. 'Aye; of that there can be nae argument, Vicar. Mr Croall always makes sure to stock up the coal at this time of year, just in case the weather takes a turn for the worse. Moving about the boiler room's like finding yer way aroun' Hampton Court Maze these days.' He laughed at his observation as he squirreled Chappelton's greatcoat into a small cloakroom area adjacent to the revolving door. 'Now, might I have the pleasure of showing ye to...'

'Ah, Reverend Chappelton!' came an enthusiastic but familiar cry from further along the corridor. Extricating himself from a small throng of well-wishers, the sprightly Mr Croall strode towards his newly-arrived guest with a youthful energy that refuted his advancing years. Sweeping up to Chappelton, the curator pumped his hand with enthusiastic vigour. 'I am elated to see you here this evening, sir. Thank you for coming.'

Bowled over by the effusiveness of his host, the vicar blinked hard. 'The pleasure is all mine, sir, I can assure you. And thank *you*, once again, for your kind invitation.'

'Think nothing of it,' said the dapper curator, waving his hand as though to dispel his guest's remark. Croall too had left no stone unturned in smartening his appearance for the evening; his evening suit immaculate and his beard neatly groomed, he looked every inch the country gentleman - and one who certainly seemed to have no shortage of guests to entertain. 'Please,' he entreated, gesturing for Chappelton to join him in moving along the hallway, 'come and join us in the reading room. There are some guests there who I have no doubt would be charmed to make your acquaintance.'

The young curate felt somewhat underdressed in his professional attire as Croall swept between clusters of well-groomed visitors with proficient poise. The curator led his guest up to a doorway next to the foyer's grandfather clock, gesturing for him to enter. The sight which met Chappelton there, however, was to catch him quite by surprise. Within the room - standing like an army of silent sentries - were row upon row of bookcases, each lined with leather-bound volumes, periodicals and magazines. The woodwork seemed to be oak; whether solid or imitation, the vicar could not say. The shelving was interspersed with large windows which, in daylight, would no doubt have well illuminated the room - but, at this hour of the evening, were instead reflective of the light emanating from a combination of wall-mounted lamps and a roaring coal fire a few feet along from the doorway. Yet it was the ceiling which drew Chappelton's eyes upwards, and which proved to be the focus of his astonishment. There, in panels demarcated in soft red and turquoise blue, were several lines of large circular portraits cast in plaster. These roundels, alternating with coats of arms, were an arresting sight, for no two figures were at all alike. Their subjects, both male and female, seemed to have been plucked from across the centuries; some appeared Mediaeval in origin, while others looked almost Classical.

'Impressive, aren't they?' came an unknown voice - one which made Chappelton suddenly aware that he'd been gawping at the striking spectacle above his head with little attentiveness towards the rest of world around him. He turned to see the cheerful face of a young man - he seemed much the same age as Chappelton himself - with a ruddy complexion and a ready smile. His suit was cut in the modern style, though his wiry form suggested someone who was just as accustomed to physical effort as he was to social pleasantries. 'They are facsimiles, of course - cast from the original Stirling Heads.'

'Stirling Heads, sir?' asked the vicar, genuinely intrigued. 'I am afraid I must confess that I am unfamiliar with the term.'

'Carved oak roundels taken from the ceiling of the King's Presence Chamber at Stirling Castle. Painted, originally... not that you'd know it now, of course, for the years have taken their toll somewhat.' The unknown guest was watching carefully for any flicker of recognition. 'They do make rather a fitting decoration for this grand library though, you must agree - even if it was not quite what the Stuart monarchs had intended, most likely. But one would never have seen their like even in the heyday of Alexandria, and in my opinion that is reason enough to appreciate their artistry.'

'Bravo, sir!' said Mr Croall, laughing gamely. 'With friends like you, I fear I shall soon be out of a job.' Turning to address the vicar, he added: 'The Reverend Sebastian Chappelton, may I introduce another of my guests this evening: Mr Joseph Denovan Adam.'

'My pleasure, Reverend,' Adam inclined his head graciously. He had an impish glint in his eye which, even in spite of his finery, reminded the vicar of a disorderly child about to go scrumping for apples. 'You are a visitor in Stirling, might I presume?'

Chappelton nodded in response. 'Yes, sir; that is correct. I am only here for a short sabbatical. Though might I discern from your own accent that you are local to the area?'

'Mr Adam runs the Craigmill Studio, a school for artists near the town,' Croall interjected helpfully. 'To say nothing of being a hugely talented painter in his own right.'

'You flatter me, Mr Croall,' said Adam with an arch smile. 'If only one of my works is remembered beyond my passing, I shall be content. But tell me, will your charming family be joining us this evening?'

Croall beamed warmly at the mention of his kin, unable to conceal his evident fondness for them - or his appreciation towards his friend's enquiry. 'Indeed they shall, sir! Annie and Margaret are through in the watercolour gallery, welcoming some of the other guests, though I regret that young Mary shall not be joining us this evening. She has a touch of fever, alas, and so Mrs Croall is watching over her bedside.'

'I am sorry to hear that,' the young artist proclaimed, his expression suddenly grave in its sincerity. 'I hope that her recovery comes swiftly.'

'As do I, sir. The doctor tells us that it is nothing that a little bed-rest won't cure in the fullness of time - though, it must be said, perhaps she was a little overcome with excitement at the arrival of Father Christmas. She is still of that age, you know - the opening of gifts is nothing less than an adventure to be relished.'

Clearing his throat as though to remind the elegantly-dressed curator of his presence, Chappelton enquired politely: 'Mary is your daughter, Mr Croall?'

'That she is, Reverend,' he replied, inclining his head subtly in acknowledgement. 'My youngest child - just turned eleven this year. Though I happily forgive your confusion, as my dear lady wife is also named Mary. I regret the fact that you will not be meeting them this evening, though of course my other two daughters will be more than delighted to greet you. Which reminds me,' he added, tugging his pocket-watch from his waistcoat and consulting it briefly, 'I must attend to the civic party. The Provost is... well, it is no secret that he is a man who does not appreciate being kept waiting. If you will excuse me please, sirs.'

With a polite nod to both Chappelton and Adam, the nimble custodian backed gently out of the reading room, neatly sidestepping a couple of official-looking gentlemen as they strode through the doorway in his wake.

Adam turned in Croall's wake, casting his gaze around the room before returning them to the vicar. 'Our host is a remarkable gentleman, Mr Chappelton, is he not? Scientist, scholar, patron of the arts... Stirling should count itself fortunate to have such ready access to the talent of one such as he.'

'One certainly cannot fault his hospitality,' the cleric responded musingly. 'It seems that he has invited me - all but a stranger - into the midst of the town's best and brightest.'

With a gentle sweep of his arm, Adam ushered Chappelton away from the door and further into the library. If the vicar had anticipated the aroma of dusty books, his expectations would have been unfounded, as he was instead met by the scent of newly-leatherbound volumes and the subtle fragrance of festive spices wafting from the foyer nearby - a welcoming touch to put the guests in the festive spirit, no doubt. Although a good number of people were attending the event, the Institute's capacious rooms never allowed these public areas to seem crowded, and the general atmosphere was one of amiable cordiality - a fact aided to no small degree by the roaring coal fire, its hearth positioned between the library's two doors, which warmed the area more than comfortably.

'Many of those in attendance are members of the Stirling Guildry and the Chamber of Trade, you know,' Adam noted by way of explanation as he and the vicar moved towards the centre of the room, 'though some are public officials of the Burgh. The Provost you will no doubt meet later, as Mr Croall suggests - indeed, I would hazard that there will be no mistaking him. But for the moment, there is someone else with whom I should be privileged to make your introduction.'

The artist stopped just short of two men who were currently deep in conversation. The first was a slightly stooped man of average height, who had dark hair and a full-bodied beard which reached some way beyond the base of his neck. Though youthful, perhaps only in his twenties, his groomed, hirsute appearance lent him an air of distinction. Dressed in a formal academic cap and gown, the attentive movement of his sharp features betrayed an insightful intelligence. Making up the other half of the discussion was a tall, distinguished-looking man in middle age with a wild shock of snowy white hair perched atop his angular head. Garbed in a dark, almost funereal suit, he peered over *pince-nez* spectacles at his discursive companion, his clean-shaven features displaying a polite but genuine curiosity towards the younger man's words.

61

Upon noticing Adam's quiet approach, the bearded gentleman coughed politely to mark an interruption in the flow of his exchange, turning slightly to consider the new arrivals. 'Well, Joseph,' the scholarly stranger declared, his voice deep but kindly, 'I see from your ecclesiastical companion that you have at last sought confession for your sins against art!'

Adam laughed heartily, his good humour seeming all too genuine. Chappelton's expression momentarily divulged his confusion over what was quite clearly a private joke, and so the jovial artist courteously noted: 'Might I present Mr Leonard Baker, art master at the High School of Stirling.' The tall man nodded in acknowledgement. 'Leonard - I have pleasure in introducing the Reverend Mr Sebastian Chappelton, Minister of...'

From the awkward silence which resulted from Adam's unintentionally-truncated introduction, the vicar surmised that his new friend was naturally curious about his place of origin, and thus quickly interjected: 'The Vicar of Whinmoor - at your service, sirs. It is but a modest parish in Yorkshire... but for me, it is home.'

'The pleasure is entirely ours, Mr Chappelton,' Baker articulated gently, the surface of his eyes sparkling in the reflective glow from the fireplace nearby. 'Always a pleasure to see a new face here at the Institute.'

'Then you are a regular visitor, I trust?' the clergyman enquired civilly.

Baker grinned broadly. 'You could put it that way, sir. Last year I was privileged to oversee a contemporary art exhibition at Mr Croall's invitation. For a few weeks I almost seemed to be a permanent resident here, but I like to think that the end result was worth the endeavour - for the public as much as for the artists involved.'

'My old friend is too diffident for his own good,' Adam interjected with ardour. 'It was the success of that very exhibition which - in some small part - inspired this evening's event, you see. None of it would have been possible without Leonard's meticulous industry.'

'Or indeed Mr Croall's patience!' the schoolmaster laughed politely. 'The amount of time I spent arranging and rearranging paintings in those galleries, I have little doubt there were times he felt like locking me in one of his display cases and throwing away the key.'

Attempting not to look too ill at ease, the white-haired gentleman next to Baker coughed meekly before uttering: '*Jawohl*, Joseph - you never did explain the reason for the gathering this evening. Some kind of annual British custom, I trust?'

The older man's voice reminded Chappelton somewhat inappropriately of a coffin lid creaking on rusty hinges, though the primary focus of his attention was the strength and distinctiveness of his Germanic accent. 'My dear Doctor,' muttered Adam, affronted at his oversight, 'please forgive my lack of etiquette. Reverend, if may introduce my guest for this evening: Dr Ernst Schottler, from the University of Heidelberg.'

'Delighted, I am sure,' the Prussian nodded, his manner formal but by no means aloof. In spite of his unmistakeably European brogue, his grasp of English was impeccable, his speech lacking any trace of hesitancy. 'It is a relief to know that I am not the only guest this evening who does not hail from Stirling.'

'Dr Schottler is a leading authority on bovine anatomy,' Baker added helpfully. 'He has kindly agreed to visit Stirling at Joseph's request, in order to assist him in his work for a short while - in an advisory capacity, you understand.'

Chappelton arched an eyebrow in surprise. 'I'm not sure I understand, Mr Adam. Bovine anatomy? Are you perchance involved in dairy farming?'

Adam chuckled easily, clearly amused by the observation. 'Well, it would certainly be one way to meet my organisation's expenditure... but no, sir; nothing quite so practical, I'm afraid. My studio operates the only artistic school in Scotland dedicated to animal artwork.' The pride in his voice was subtle but more than evident. 'I have expended many years in my pursuit of depicting the beasts of the field with style and accuracy, but nothing has come to fascinate me quite so much as the complexity of the animals' complex bone structure and musculature. Quite fascinating, actually. To this end, Dr Schottler has very kindly agreed to offer me scholarly guidance on faithfully representing the anatomical intricacy of these creatures - adding an extra layer of truthfulness to the artistry, if you will.'

'I cannot help but commend you on the diligence of your artistic endeavours, sir,' Schottler noted unassumingly, 'but you greatly flatter my reputation. I am but a humble *Tierarzt* who has been fortunate enough to have my peers take note of my chaotic scribblings. And besides, it is I who should be thanking *you* - I have always dearly wished to see the rolling hills of Scotland, even when I was but a child back in Saxony.'

'Will you be staying in the country long, Doctor...?' asked Baker, before allowing his question to trail off into silence. The reason for his self-imposed interruption, Chappelton soon discovered, was due to the emergence of a new figure into the reading room - and one which demanded immediate attention. An immaculately-groomed gentleman of medium build strode through the main door from the foyer, dressed in full academic regalia. The tassel of his mortar board danced behind his head as he forged his way through the throng, though Chappelton almost felt as though the newcomer's natural air of cerebral authority was causing the crowd to split before him like a latter-day parting of the Red Sea. The vicar believed the learned gentleman to be of perhaps the same age as himself, though the prematurely-greying hair of his waxed moustache made him seem slightly older than his years. Driving forwards toward their position like an unstoppable force of nature, the man seemed more like a regimental sergeant major than a scholar, and Chappelton found himself eyeing the advancing visitor somewhat warily.

'Mr Baker,' the cultured man snapped curtly, his voice ringing out like a bullet in the night. 'I see that your punctuality is beyond reproach this evening.'

'Thank you, Rector,' Baker responded, his tone neutral.

The haughty newcomer gazed at his colleague disdainfully. 'A pity that it is a phenomenon rarely repeated during working hours,' he contributed with some degree of dramatic flourish, though his aloof demeanour suggested that it was meant only partially in jest. 'Still, you are present as required, for which I am grateful.'

Keen to break the unnerving silence which followed, the art master tentatively enquired: 'Your journey here was a pleasant one, might I assume?'

'Adequate, Baker... if only just,' the stranger scoffed, his derision almost tangible. 'I cannot abide the sense of laxity at this time of year. Give people a religious festival and everything seems to go to seed these days. The next thing you know, they shall be looking for an excuse to make it a public holiday.'

'Perish the thought,' Adam muttered dryly. 'It is a great relief to observe that your manifest fervour for the festive season has not diminished now that St Stephen's has been and gone, sir.'

Whether he heard the barbed implication lodged within the comment or not, the stern scholar decided to steamroller on anyway. 'And now there's this evening's... *frivolity*.' He spat the word out as though it was an obscenity. 'It is often said that these civic social events are like marrying into the aristocracy - the honour is invariably greater than the pleasure. One moment I am enjoying the comfort of hearth and home, a trusted volume of Aristotle by my side, the next I'm surrounded by these confounded plaster-cast facsimiles; as if the genuine Stirling Heads were not decoration enough for one building. But still, one's duty is one's duty, I'm sure you will agree.'

Wisely deciding not to engage with this particular line of enquiry, Baker instead turned to the others and announced, 'Gentlemen, might I introduce Mr...'

'Andrew Fleming Hutchison, Master of Arts,' the headmaster interrupted brusquely, the laboured emphasis on his academic title speaking volumes to Chappelton. 'I am in charge of the High School of Stirling, and by that same token the man responsible for educating the youth of this town.' He flicked his eyes momentarily between the men arranged around the library fireplace, his mildly condescending expression suggesting that he was sizing them up for a possible detention. 'Mr Joseph Denovan Adam, I know by reputation. However,' he said, turning on

67

his heel to face Chappelton and Schottler more directly, 'I fail to recognise either of you gentlemen. Might I presume you are new to the area?'

Schottler eyed the spirited headteacher with what seemed to be a mixture of awe and quizzicality. 'It would perhaps be more accurate to say that we are but visitors to Stirling, sir. My name is Dr Ernst Schottler, and I am *Hochschullehrer* in animal physiology at der Universität Heidelberg.'

Hutchison nodded approvingly, showing more enthusiasm than he had since entering the library. 'A fellow scholar - excellent, sir. Yes, excellent! I hope you would perhaps see fit to join us for a visit of our own educational establishment. I am always eager to hear new theories, to compare approaches and so forth.'

'Stirling is, of course, forever indebted to Germany for the arrival of the Burgh's first Christmas tree,' Baker ventured meekly. 'I was just mentioning to Dr Schottler that the custom was introduced to the town by the High School's Mr Roeding in the winter of '55, and of the delight of all the...'

The headmaster seemed a trifle piqued at the interruption, and thus promptly made one of his own. 'Indeed, yes - that festive evergreen. Merely a passing fad, no doubt. As though there were not distractions enough at this time of year.' His comportment suggested that the adopted tradition did not exactly enthuse him, to say the least. 'I should be rather more interested to know the good Doctor's opinions on the recent Dual Alliance between his country and Austria-Hungary. It seems that we live in interesting times, does it not?'

'With respect, Mr Hutchison,' Schottler offered, a slight edge creeping into his voice, 'I think it inappropriate to discuss matters of foreign policy in public. Is it not said that gentlemen never discuss politics or religion?'

'Poppycock!' the rector boomed, the tonality of his voice suggesting that a demand for a hundred lines was not too far away. 'Gentlemen discuss little else, Herr Doktor... with the singular exception, perhaps, of money. And you, sir,' he added, turning his attention to Chappelton. 'Am I to deduce that you are also a guest in our fair town?'

Unsure of the best way to react to the headteacher's overbearing manner, the vicar kept the modulation of his voice carefully dispassionate as he replied: 'One who is perhaps an even more temporary visitor than Dr Schottler here, it is true. But yes; I have that honour, sir.'

'An Englishman, upon my soul!' exclaimed Hutchison. 'Well, I do hope that you are enjoying your stay here in Stirling. We might not have the Anglican pomp and ceremony that you're used to at home... but then again, given the recent upheaval of the establishment in the south I rather imagine you would be forgiven for desiring the occasional break from all the endless debates.'

'You refer, I presume, to the Public Worship Regulation Act?' Chappelton asked cautiously. 'As with so many areas of intersection between politics and theology, there are... well, some areas of negotiation which need to be explored. Though as I'm sure you can imagine, there have been many vigorous disputes these past few years.'

'And a great many more to come, no doubt. Not that the Act has any application here in Scotland, of course, though the arcane disputes surrounding the finer points of ritual are always of passing interest.' Strangely enough, the rector's expression seemed anything but absorbed by the potential of further discussion on the matter, but he ploughed on nonetheless. 'So what brings you to Stirling in particular? Keen to visit the home of the Drummond Tract Depot, no doubt?'

Chappelton frowned, the name vaguely familiar to him and yet... in spite of himself, he could not place it. 'Drummond Tract Depot, sir? A publishing firm local to the area, am I to assume?'

'Publishing firm?' Hutchison spluttered, his reaction suggesting that the vicar had just kicked him in the shin. 'The Drummond company's religious tracts are known in the furthest corners of the Empire, sir! Indeed, the prolificacy of their output is nothing short of staggering.'

'Forgive me,' Chappelton muttered. 'My mind has been rather preoccupied of late.'

The headmaster snorted. 'Preoccupied, you say? An excuse I hear all too often from pupils who have forgotten their homework.' Sweeping his hand theatrically around the room's numerous stacked shelves, he added: 'It seems to me, sir, that your time may be better served reading books instead of merely standing in their presence.'

Riled by the older man's bluster, Adam's eyes narrowed. 'Mr Hutchison, need I remind you that you are addressing a man of the cloth - to say nothing of a guest in our town? I suggest that you apologise immediately.'

'Mmm,' grumbled Hutchison, pausing rather sullenly before he grudgingly offered: 'Perhaps I did speak in haste, Reverend. I must confess that my zeal for the written word does, on occasion, incline me towards a lack of diplomacy. Call it a scholar's indulgence, if you will.'

The fact was not lost on Chappelton, of course, that no actual apology had been forthcoming.

As the conversation trailed off inelegantly, the vicar could not fail to notice the way in which the yellow-orange glare of the fire reflected against the gold-leaf lettering etched upon the spines of the library's many leather-bound volumes. The effect of radiated warmth seemed quite in contrast to the frosty tone of the discussion since Hutchison's arrival. Baker was looking around uncomfortably, reluctant to reignite the exchange after his superior's social *faux-pas*, while Schottler seemed to be intent upon watching the non-verbal cues between the group, almost as though studying their interactions as he might one of his laboratory experiments. Before anyone had the opportunity to speak again, however, the grandfather clock in the reception area could be heard chiming the hour, leading to a renewed murmur of anticipation throughout the assembled gathering in the reading room.

Saved by the bell, the vicar thought - immediately suspecting that more than one of his companions was sharing the very same notion.

'Gentlemen,' said Adam, his usual enthusiastic comportment now tinged with a degree of lassitude due to his present company (it seemed to Chappelton's ears at least). 'It appears that the appointed time is now at hand. I think perhaps we should adjourn to the galleries, and see for ourselves exactly what surprise Mr Croall has summoned us to witness this evening.'

CHAPTER III
Pictures at an Exhibition

The lower gallery seemed somehow different to the Reverend Chappelton upon his entry into the spacious, painting-bedecked area. Initially he believed the change was attributable to the animated bustle of guests milling around the room's carefully-populated walls; when his earlier visit had taken place, it had seen the room devoid of inhabitants save for Mr McLafferty and himself. Yet it was recollecting the dimness of the room during the onset of dusk that previous day which alerted him to the true fact behind the gallery's transformation: large portable lamps had been wheeled into the room to illuminate the area, casting an inviting glow which bathed the various frames and canvases in a temperate and restful light.

Chappelton felt relieved to have slipped away from his previous partners in conversation. Although Adam and Baker had seemed amiable enough company, the vicar had found the scholarly Hutchison's brash, almost strident manner somewhat unpalatable. Given the number of guests in attendance, he felt sure that his absence from their company would not be missed - or, more to the point, seem in any way discourteous.

His new-found solitary status afforded him the opportunity to study the gallery's watercolours in detail for the first time; weaving in and out of the various clusters of patrons, he was able now to appreciate the many paintings on display with greater ease. Rural churches and ruined castles jockeyed for position alongside sheep grazing upon pastoral landscapes, rolling hills and wispy cloud formations, and more than a few instances of still life. The constant juxtaposition of styles and subjects never ceased to impress Chappelton, who found himself developing a heightened awareness for the skill of the brush-stroke.

One particular watercolour drew his eye, however. It depicted a cavern of some sort, dimly lit from the artist's point of view and yet, in its suggestion of depth, gradually appearing darker and more shadowy the farther one peered into it. The effect, the parson became all too aware, was actually rather mesmerising. The ethereal scene appeared redolent of mystery and the unknown, and in a strange way it also recalled to his memory the philosopher Plato's famous Parable of the Cave.

'An impressive piece, is it not?'

The vicar slowly turned to appraise the source of a new voice, its enunciation self-assured but yet strangely delicate. Its source, though her approach had been all but soundless, was a bespectacled lady who looked to be in her late sixties. The woman was dressed entirely in black, her taste in clothing somewhat too conservative for the modern fashion, and though short in stature she possessed an undeniable presence which was entirely at odds with her unprepossessing appearance. Initially, the cleric assumed her to be a grieving widow, and yet there was a fire in her eyes that spoke less of mourning and more of steely determination.

'I must have visited this gallery dozens of times since the Institute opened its doors, you know, and yet I never grow tired of the sheer variety on display.' Her eyes seemed to take in many things simultaneously, Chappelton noticed, flicking between the artistic subjects of the paintings and the activity of the room at large.

Taken aback by the forthright woman's intensity, the curate offered: 'One cannot fail to be struck by the artist's impressive employment of light.'

'And also darkness,' the vaguely Sibylline lady replied, her tone of voice remaining resolutely matter-of-fact. 'This particular work was painted by the founder of this Institute, Thomas Stuart Smith. *A Cave*, he entitled it. You will find many similarly impressive pieces by him on display around the galleries - some of them with considerably more imaginative titles. But then, artistic appreciation is of course the goal of this event, is it not?'

'So I am led to believe,' Chappelton noted noncommittally.

'I understand that Mr Croall is paying host to a guest exhibition this evening, though if he is following the same procedure as last year's event the display will be situated through in the upper gallery... which, I presume, is why the door is currently locked. All things in time, as they say; no doubt a short speech or two will be in order before we shall be allowed to peruse the works which have been offered up for view.' The latter prospect appeared to enthuse her considerably less than the former.

Looking over his shoulder, the vicar noted the accuracy of the woman's observation; the large double-doors leading to the main gallery were indeed closed and locked, as was the adjacent passageway through to the upper museum. It seemed, he could only assume, that Mr Croall was planning a very particular course of events for his guests this evening, and that the temporary exhibition that Baker had fleetingly mentioned was yet to play its part.

'It seems that you know the ways of our host well, Mrs...?'

'MacLagan,' the conservatively-dressed lady answered. 'Miss Christian MacLagan. And yes, I count Alexander Croall both a friend and a colleague in science, though I am sure that you will not have heard of me personally,' she stated quite bluntly. 'I am an archaeologist, antiquarian, historian... in truth, there are many fields of knowledge in which I have involved myself.'

'That you are noted in your disciplines, madam, I do not dispute,' Chappelton responded politely.

'On the contrary,' MacLagan shot back, her voice controlled and yet tinged with acid. 'You are undoubtedly wondering how a "mere woman" may claim to have any kind of standing in any of these areas of expertise. Indeed, no doubt you have taken me for some sort of gentrified dilettante whose only contribution to science has come from offering financial support to the research of others. Let me assure you that this is not so.'

The vicar reacted curiously, unsure exactly how his prickly new acquaintance expected him to respond. 'Upon my word, Miss MacLagan, I can assure you that no such thought entered my mind.'

'No, of course not,' she muttered, though her general bearing suggested that she believed quite the opposite. 'But even if so, you would not have been the first person tonight to remind me that I am but an *associate* member of the Society of Antiquaries, even in spite of my substantial body of work. Books, papers, my breadth of study on Neolithic monuments... what does any of it matter, they claim, when I would be better suited to needlepoint and serving high tea, hmm?'

Increasingly uncertain of how to handle MacLagan's fiery temperament, the vicar swallowed hard. 'Please do not despair. If recognition of your efforts may appear to be in vain amongst men, at least bear in mind that all is known to Almighty God. He at least appreciates the depth of your knowledge and perspicuous commitment to your field.'

'Do you honestly think me unaware of that fact?' she smiled wanly, the gesture seeming somewhat bitter. 'I have been a member of the Free Church ever since the Disruption, sir. And I tell you that if the Lord gave me the skill and understanding to advance my studies in my field of research, He would not have intended for me to hide that light under a bushel. Or am I wrong, Mr Chappelton?'

The inquisitive clergyman was momentarily startled at the sound of his name. 'Do forgive me, madam, but I am afraid that you seem to have me at a disadvantage. Have we by some chance met before?'

'Not at all,' MacLagan noted, her tone still clipped. 'I couldn't help but overhear part of your conversation through in the reading room. Indeed, with Mr Hutchison's clarity of voice I feel certain that certain members of the Nova Scotia Chamber of Trade were privy to it also.'

'Indeed, yes,' Chappelton nodded cautiously. 'The rector does appear to be a man with great enthusiasm for his work,' he added with supreme diplomacy.

'That's just the thing, sir. The man is brilliant - quite brilliant. A prolific scholar of noted precision, he is a polymath of quite extraordinary talent and breadth of knowledge. The High School could not ask for a steadier hand at its helm.' The vicar waited for the inevitable qualifier in this veritable cavalcade of grudging praise. 'However,' MacLagan added with considerably greater passion, 'he would

78

do well to remember that he is not always in charge of a classroom full of unruly children. His theatrics so very often obscure his intellectual brilliance. But then, I must confess, there are a great many areas where he and I have not been in accord over the years.'

Given the spirited lady's firebrand nature, Chappelton did not doubt the veracity of her statement - or that her free-thinking mind was likely often at odds with orthodox opinion. Keen to steer the conversation onto a less confrontational path, however, he instead offered: 'Mr Baker tells me that last year witnessed a very successful art exhibition here. Is tonight to see another such event?'

'You refer, I presume, to the educational art exhibition? Yes, I understand that another similar occasion is to be arranged, though it may be a few years away yet. This evening, on the other hand, is merely inspired by that previous impressive exposition, and is apparently on a considerably more modest scale.' She shifted her weight slightly, again surveying the room as though looking for a particular face in the crowd. 'There is to be a small guest exhibition, I am told, though largely comprised of artwork loaned to the Institute from other establishments - alongside that of new artists, of course.'

'An excellent way of involving the local community in the Institute's services,' Chappelton observed.

'And, of course, it provides a golden opportunity to invite donations from the public, so that other such proceedings may take place in future. The main event of the evening, on the other hand, has been shrouded in secrecy. From what I can gather, it seems that Mr Croall and the Provost are the only ones present who have any knowledge of it.'

'Very intriguing,' the vicar noted softly. 'He hinted as much the other day, though only obliquely. I do wonder what our host has in store for us?'

'Something unexpected, sir,' came a new voice, and one with an unmistakeable ring of self-importance. 'Of that there can be no doubt. If there is one thing that I have discovered about the Smith Institute this evening, it is that it is *full* of surprises.'

The commanding intonation belonged to a large, heavy-set man wearing an army officer's dress uniform. From the way that he was in the process of bustling past them, Chappelton had the unmistakeable sense that this martial gentleman's interjection had come more as a passing aside than a premeditated interruption. He was tall and somewhat ungainly, his bulk suggesting that he had been hewn from a slab of granite. Appearing to be in his early to mid-fifties, he sported a neatly-combed mop of thick ginger hair framing affable features which tapered to an impeccably-trimmed beard.

MacLagan, faultlessly sharp-eyed as always, was taking careful note of the rank insignia on the newcomer's epaulettes. 'On that point, Major, we are in agreement. You are, I trust, a visitor to the town like the Reverend here?'

'In a manner of speaking, madam,' he bowed respectfully, 'though on a matter of business rather than pleasure. I am afraid I can speak no more of it.' He tapped his nose in a gesture of secrecy which, Chappelton could tell from her reaction, MacLagan found impossibly condescending. 'My name is Major Angus Campbell, of the 93rd Highland Regiment.' His voice carried an unmistakeable Highland burr, almost suggestive of the Western Isles.

'Barracked at the Castle, might I presume?' Chappelton enquired.

'Just so, sir,' the officer nodded approvingly. 'An invitation was issued to the Colonel, in point of fact, though regrettably he was unable to attend due to matters outwith his control. I must say, however, that his loss was most certainly my gain. The hospitality this evening has been unimpeachable.'

'No doubt a welcome departure from your usual duties, Major,' MacLagan observed perceptively. 'I see from your array of medals that you are a veteran of the Crimean campaign. Sebastopol is no small distance from Stirling, after all; in fact, I do believe that some of your colleagues brought Russian cannon back with them to prove exactly that point.'

Campbell responded with impressed surprise at her knowledge of the decorations pinned to his dress uniform. 'You are remarkably observant, madam, if I may say. Though alas, I was but a junior officer back then, and my part in our nation's victory was far from covered in glory.'

'You were wounded in battle, perhaps?' the vicar asked carefully.

'Injured, perhaps, but by no means conventionally. Let's just say that God was looking out for me when we faced the Russians at Inkerman, Reverend. On the field of battle I was kicked by a horse when it was startled by enemy artillery.' He shuddered at the memory, even from all those years ago. 'It wouldn't have seemed so bad, you see, were it not for the fact that it was one of our own mounted cavalry division that did the damage. So there I was, a young Second Lieutenant readied for battle, having to be stretchered from the combat zone on account of a broken leg and dislocated jaw. A fine example *that* set for the men, let me tell you.'

MacLagan pursed her lips thoughtfully. 'The main thing, one would suppose, is that you survived the conflict at all. I'm led to believe that more Russians died getting to the Crimea than actually perished in the warzone.'

'If I might venture, madam, I should have been just as happy if they had remained at home. It may well have saved us all a lot of time and trouble.' Campbell cleared his throat, seemingly eager to put past traumas behind him. 'And speaking of time, I find myself asking when we shall have the pleasure of our host's company again. One cannot be less than intrigued by his taste for the cloak and dagger.' The officer nodded across to the opposite side of the room, where two smartly-dressed young women were welcoming new guests into the gallery. 'The curator's charming daughters have just been telling me that the details of the evening's main event are about to be unveiled. But I must confess to some curiosity, for they seemed unusually tight-lipped about the issue.'

Chappelton could not deny that Croall's progeny were indeed a credit to him. Flawlessly mannered, they greeted the Institute's guests with a warmth and charm to rival their father's unfaultable conviviality. There seemed to be little difference in the ages of the young women - and yet although both were clearly in their mid-twenties, their individual deportment could not have been less similar. The elder of the two - who, from the curator's earlier description, Chappelton took to be Margaret - had a refined elegance about her movements, with classically attractive features and an affectionate but ultimately rather timid, self-effacing manner. Her sister, by contrast, seemed considerably more bookish in her appearance, her glasses and serious expression lending her an undeniably studious air which had much in common with her father. This, he took to be Annie. Yet for all of her intellectually sophisticated countenance she could not disguise a charismatic demeanour and sharp wit; in the short period that he had observed her, Chappelton noted

83

her effortless ability to put visitors at ease, or to engender a warm smile on this cold winter's night.

'Well, whatever spectacle Mr Croall has planned, I hope that he will be bringing it about sooner rather than later,' MacLagan noted waspishly. 'We have witnessed many arrivals this evening, but little action thus far.'

Campbell laughed lightly, his medals jangling on his chest. 'A fair observation - if, I might submit, one which may be accused of lacking in tact.'

'Should you have the good fortune to reach my age, Major, I think you will discover that tact is merely an impediment to plain speaking - and much time is subsequently wasted because of it.' She cleared her throat, glanced at a delicate gold wristwatch, and then tutted loudly. 'And furthermore, sir, in your profession you may do well to...'

'Ladies and gentlemen, may I have your attention please!' From the doorway to the foyer, the Christmas tree candles twinkling behind him, the sudden reappearance of Mr Croall curtailed Miss MacLagan's castigatory musings in a heartbeat. Spreading his arms, the building's custodian addressed the room with great passion, the unvarnished enthusiasm in his voice already proving quite infectious. 'My name is Alexander Croall, curator of this building and its collections, and it is my pleasure to welcome you all to the Smith Institute this evening. Later, I will have the honour of introducing you to a selection of paintings which have been loaned to us for a brief period, via special agreement with their owners, for your viewing delectation.' A ripple of appreciation, mixed with genuine curiosity, spread throughout the room. 'But first, I would invite you to join me in the lower museum for a most special unveiling by the Provost of the Burgh of Stirling, Mr George Christie. While I apologise for the delay, I can assure each of you in advance that none shall be disappointed.'

* * *

It soon occurred to Chappelton that the lower museum was the only public area in the Institute to which he had not hitherto been introduced. As he filed in alongside the other guests, he realised in hindsight that Mr Croall had studiously avoided access to the room during his earlier visit, and - dominating the centre of floor - he quickly discerned why that may have been the case. What appeared to be a display cabinet of moderate size, perhaps five and a half feet tall by three feet in width and breadth, stood prominently in the midpoint of the room, a large dust cover obscuring its contents from view.

Standing next to the exhibit case was a stout man with staid, humourless features. Though not an especially tall individual, he nevertheless exuded an impression of dour presence which distinguished him from the room's other inhabitants. Clean shaven, his expression was severe, and Chappelton did not need the visual cue of his chains of office to identify the man as the Provost of Stirling. In middle age, the hair around his temples starting to grey, there was no denying his natural ease of authority, and his obvious comfort in the public eye suggested to the vicar that this particular Provost had held council office for some considerable time.

As he politely manoeuvred his way around the room to find a decent vantage point for the unveiling, Chappelton could not help but be impressed by the arrangement of historical items that Mr Croall had put on display around the rest of the room. Indeed, it felt almost unfair that the covered exhibit was drawing all eyes when there were so many other curiosities and objects of interest to view. Unlike the upper museum, with its seamlessly-organised array of exhibits from across the globe, the contents of this room seemed to be entirely comprised of items of Scottish ethnographic origin, most of them appearing to derive from the annals of the country's complex social history. The walls of the lower museum shared the same grey, neutral colour scheme of their larger neighbour, but circling them - spaced around at regular intervals - were none other than the oak roundels of the genuine Stirling Heads. Chappelton found these striking originals to be even more remarkable in their detail than the plaster replicas which decorated the reading room, and voiced unspoken appreciation that they had - against all odds - managed to survive the ravages of history.

Within a short time, the museum hall was full almost to capacity as guests politely filtered in through the door to witness the Institute's star attraction for the evening. Not for the first time, Chappelton found himself impressed by just how many visitors were in attendance, not least by the sheer number who managed to fit comfortably within the lower museum's confines. Over in the corner, he could see the incomparable Andrew Hutchison continuing to lord it over an increasingly beleaguered Leonard Baker, while Dr Schottler and Joseph Denovan Adam were chatting amiably with Colonel Campbell. Miss MacLagan was engaged in what seemed to be an uncharacteristically genial conversation with the elder of Mr Croall's two daughters, while her somewhat more diffident younger sister stood by the doorway watching proceedings in silent consideration.

As the crowd settled down amongst the assorted display cabinets, the curator quietly made his way to the covered central case, Mr McLafferty not far from his side. Sensing the assembled visitors' anticipation, he wasted no time in clearing his throat in order to call the room to silence. 'Ladies and gentlemen,' Croall announced deferentially. 'May I present the Provost of Stirling, Mr George Christie.'

Taking a respectful step backwards, symbolically vacating centre stage in favour of the Provost, Croall removed himself by a few steps just as Christie made his way into a position just in front of the teasingly-obscured case. He tugged on his lapels, the burnished metal of his official chains sparkling in the reflected glow of the room's wall-mounted lighting emplacements. 'Thank you, Mr Croall,' he said, his piercing voice carrying to every corner of the room. Everything from his stance to his polished delivery marked him out as a highly experienced public speaker. 'And thank you, one and all, for joining us on what I hope will prove to be a most auspicious occasion.

'1879 has been a noteworthy year for us here in Stirling, and for two particular reasons. Firstly, it marks ten years since the death of this building's founder, the late Mr Thomas Stuart Smith. Some of you may have known Mr Smith in his lifetime. Indeed, I myself counted him as a friend. But though we may never again know his quick wit and extensive artistic skill, we do have this building to forever remember his legacy to the people of Stirling. Here, the genius of his artistry will live on for future generations - and may no-one seek to deny its riches to our fair Burgh.

'This brings me to the second of my points of interest. The past year has marked another important occasion - namely, the commemoration of five very successful years of the Smith Institute since its grand opening to the public, under the auspices of its curator, the renowned Mr Croall. As many of you will be aware, that year of 1874 was something of a landmark for new institutions in our United

Kingdom. In London, it led to the opening of the wonderful Clockmakers' Museum. More locally, of course, we shall remember it for the equally significant establishment of the Stirling and Bridge of Allan Tramways. But we are, I have no doubt, all grateful that the Smith Institute has already proven itself to be something of a jewel in Stirling's crown, and its reputation has continued to go from strength to strength thanks to the unstinting efforts of Mr Croall's curatorship. I for one would like to wish him every success for his next five years of service to Stirling and her community.'

The thundering applause which punctuated the Provost's speech at this point left Chappelton in no doubt as to the strength of feeling which accompanied Alexander Croall's custodianship of this much-loved building, or the sheer height of the regard in which he personally was held. Though abstemious to the last in any display of pride, at least to surface observation, it was not difficult to detect that the curator was deeply moved by the sincerity of the appreciation. Christie waited patiently for the ovation to fade naturally before he continued his speech.

'A landmark date requires an equally special celebration. And so it is that tonight, in the dying days of this eventful year, that I have much pleasure in welcoming you to an event which - it is my belief - will resonate for many a decade in the annals of this fine institution.'

With a somewhat melodramatic gesture, the Provost took a side-step from his position in front of the concealed display case, motioning McLafferty to finally remove its brown sackcloth cover. The museum assistant glanced momentarily at Croall for confirmation, receiving a firm nod of approval, before pulling the sheet back in one fluid action. In so doing, he revealed a panelled glass display area atop a painted wooden plinth, its panes arranged almost as though forming a transparent cube which allowed its contents to be viewed from every direction. But it was the item within the case which elicited more than a few gasps of awe from the assembled crowd of observers.

In the centre of the secure container, resting on top of a small padded cushion, was quite the largest emerald that Chappelton had ever seen. Though he could by no means count himself an expert in mineralogy, the gleaming jewel - with its shining contours and mesmerising refracted light - had to be, at the very least, around the size of a young woman's clenched fist. Even from the far side of the room, the exhibit seemed ideally situated to dominate the lower museum, its Delphian mystique captivating the attention of the Institute's audience for the evening.

'Ladies and gentlemen,' Christie enunciated with no small amount of satisfaction, 'may I present to you the Maharajah's Homunculus.' Even the Provost himself appeared impressed by the emerald's incontestable ability to captivate the bystander's eye. 'If I might invite Mr Croall to say a few words about the star attraction of this special evening?'

Seeming eager to expound upon the precious stone's significance, the energetic curator smartly stepped up to the display case to address the assembled onlookers. 'Each of you this evening has the pleasure of being among the first men and women in Stirling to cast your eyes upon a truly remarkable exhibit. The emerald within this case is the property of His Majesty the Maharajah of Patiala, who has kindly agreed to loan it to the Smith Institute for a limited period. The Maharajah has done so in the furtherance of closer cultural ties between our two nations, but I can assure you that the timing of its presence here on this auspicious occasion is no coincidence.'

As someone who could remember all too vividly the newspaper reports regarding the Indian Rebellion of 1857 during the years of his youth, Chappelton felt certain that the goal of achieving a lasting and mutual understanding between the Empire and its overseas territories could only be regarded as a laudable one. By noticing Provost Christie subconsciously straightening his posture at this particular juncture, the vicar felt himself inclined to believe that the town council's role in the emerald's arrival was soon to be revealed.

'Weighing almost two hundred carats, and measuring very nearly three inches in diameter, the emerald is one of the largest of its kind known to exist in the world today. And yet, ladies and gentlemen, it would not be on display to you here in Stirling were it not for the efforts of our town's Provost - and one of the Smith Institute's most steadfast supporters - Mr George Christie.' Croall politely nodded at the aforementioned official, taking a half-step back as the gathered crowd broke into a short burst of heartfelt applause. Christie, his features stoical as ever, received the display of approval with quiet grace.

Courteous to a fault, the curator waited for the brief ovation to die down before continuing. 'Without the Provost's confidential negotiations with Her Imperial Majesty's representatives in India, this artefact would never have been seen outside of its native land. Indeed, only a handful of people knew that its loan would be granted until this very evening. However, in recognition of Stirling's proud history as a garrison town these past two centuries and more, it is our great honour that the Maharajah has seen fit to loan it to the Institute for this, our fifth anniversary celebration.

'The Homunculus emerald will only be on display here for a brief period - and, I must add, such is its value that it shall be guarded day and night by armed personnel during its tenure on the premises. It is our proud hope that when word is released to the public of its presence - and I do believe, in fact, that a reporter from the *Stirling Observer* is here this evening with exactly that intent - this gemstone will draw visitors from Falkirk, Perth, Glasgow... possibly even as far as Edinburgh. But this evening, I am pleased to say, each and every one of you gathered here in this room are among the very first to know of its presence in the town of Stirling.'

Chappelton was certain that he could hear a sharp, collective intake of breath sporadically taking place around the room as the assembled ladies and gentlemen of the Burgh cast their gaze upon the exceptional emerald. It was, certainly in his estimation, quite the largest precious stone that he had ever encountered... even if, by his own admission, his experience of the field was generally somewhat limited. Yet as an astute judge of character - or so he had always believed - the vicar could not entirely dissuade himself from wondering if the refracted light from the jewel was entirely responsible for the hint of green that he saw glimmering in the eyes of many among the congregated spectators inhabiting the museum that evening.

CHAPTER IV
The Shadow in the Gallery

'The Provost's doing, my foot,' spluttered Major Campbell as he took a hearty bite from his mincemeat pie. 'That emerald is here in Stirling solely in recognition of the work of Her Majesty's Armed Forces - not the finagling of provincial bureaucrats! Why else would they choose to site it in a garrison town?'

'It is laudable that you should hold your regiment's honour in such high esteem,' Joseph Denovan Adam muttered placatingly, 'but in our current company I think it perhaps more prudent that you keep such views to yourself, my good sir.'

As the officer grumbled in grudging acquiescence, the Reverend Chappelton wondered whether Campbell's outspoken bravado may have been explained by the fact that his ruminations were currently being drowned out to all but those closest to him. This welcome distraction was due to the cheerful singing of a choir of carollers who had been invited to the upper gallery at Mr Croall's invitation. The parson had earlier overhead Miss MacLagan enlightening Dr Schottler that the eight-strong ensemble comprised regular attendees at the nearby Church of the Holy Rude, whose tuneful renderings of traditional

Christmas songs had very much put them in popular demand around the Burgh at this time of year.

As far as the target of the Major's vitriol was concerned, Chappelton could see no sign of the Provost anywhere in the room, leading him to the inevitable conclusion that he must have stayed behind in the lower museum with their host when the guests had been invited to enjoy refreshments in the previously-locked main gallery. The vicar found himself questioning whether this gentle but brisk encouragement to move away from the museum was due to the fact that Mr Croall had been keen to ensure that the Institute's temporary star artefact did not overshadow the other focus of the evening, namely the visiting exhibition which was currently spread along the gallery's expansive south-facing wall. Portable lamp emplacements cast flickering light high up the walls of the room as the wooden buttresses reflected in cathedral-like splendour, their warm hue contrasting sharply with the inky darkness of night visible through the expansive panels of glass situated all along the length of the roof.

Noticing that a few of the paintings seemed familiar to him from his previous visit, Chappelton could not help but draw the conclusion that the process of briefly displacing the gallery's resident features for these new, interim attractions must have been one which had taken several days - and considerable care on the part of the curator and his assistant. Not for the first time, he was struck by the multiplicity of subject matter on display, ranging from animal art all the way through to architectural studies, conventional portraiture, and the occasional rural vista. Hanging alongside the loaned paintings, the work of local artists provided ample proof that Stirling itself had no shortage of creative talent - a factor that could not have been hampered by the encouragement of teachers so skilful as the likes of Adam and Baker.

The visual artwork, however, was not the only new feature of the upper gallery that night. True to form, Mr Croall had been responsible for a most abundant spread, a prodigious selection of sweetmeats distributed across a number of neatly-covered trestle tables for the enjoyment of the evening's guests. The festive season was represented by a huge plum pudding, which took centre stage amongst many other treats including cranberry muffins, wine jelly, apricot sherbet, and what Chappelton had been reliably informed by Margaret Croall was her mother's famous seed cake, baked according to an old family recipe. He only felt regret that their munificent host was not present to enjoy the fruits of the Institute's generosity for himself; even Mr McLafferty had returned to his customary position at the building's main doorway with the utmost of reluctance, his vigilance to the prospect of uninvited guests overruling his sweet tooth in the end.

The choir were just finishing a rousing and most harmonious rendition of 'God Rest Ye Merry Gentlemen' to enthusiastic applause from the crowd when Campbell, his mincemeat pie now long since condemned to the annals of memory, absent-mindedly brushed some crumbs of pastry from his moustache and cleared his throat politely. 'Well, gentlemen, it has been a pleasure to make your acquaintance this night. Truly, your company has made an interesting evening all the more memorable.'

Leonard Baker frowned in confusion. 'Surely, sir, you are not contemplating a departure at this early hour? Why, with our host's bounty here to enjoy - to say nothing of the fruits of Stirling's artistic labour on display - I should have thought you might wish to stay awhile longer.'

The Major smiled cryptically at the observation, seeming touched at the sincerity of the schoolmaster's sentiment. 'Your concern is much appreciated, sir - as has been the hospitality of your fellow townsfolk. But it seems that you misunderstand me. It is duty that calls for my early exit, not merely my own whim.'

'You are needed back at the Castle, perhaps?' asked Chappelton.

'Not so, Reverend. As it happens, this evening my regimental responsibilities are to take place somewhat closer at hand.'

Adam seemed amused by the officer's almost theatrical evasiveness. 'You seem

97

remarkably reticent for one who is normally so candid, Major. One would almost think you were on some kind of mission.'

'Mission?' coughed Campbell, appearing to stifle a laugh. 'Nothing quite so dramatic, Mr Adam. I'm sorry to inform you that my duties are somewhat less exotic. You will recall Mr Croall's words that the Homunculus emerald must be kept under guard at all times?' He paused momentarily for general murmurs of agreement before continuing: 'Well, as a trained and armed officer of the Realm, I will be overseeing its safety this evening until relieved by others of my regiment. After all, one must lighten the burden on Mr Croall, who is watching over the exhibit as we speak - far be it from me, after all, to deprive such a joyously festive event of its host for too long.'

Turning towards the gallery's main door, the Major made his departure, only stopping briefly to thank the cluster of sociable well-wishers once more for their conversation. Once he had gone, however, Adam's brow creased in confusion. 'What a remarkable fellow,' he declared wistfully. 'And come to think of it, what a curious assignment.'

'Whatever do you mean, Joseph?' Baker asked, seeming more bemused by his friend's comments than the unconventional manners of the departing officer.

'The 93rd Highlanders send an officer of no minor rank as their representative, on an evening dedicated to the celebration of the Burgh, its council and the Smith Institute...

and yet we discover that he is now to perform a duty - guarding a precious item - which is perhaps more befitting of an enlisted man. The whole thing seems a dashed odd state of affairs, if you ask me.'

'I think perhaps you are underestimating the ebb and flow of local politics, Mr Adam,' came a kindly new voice from nearby. Collectively, the group of men turned to see Miss Annie Croall approaching their position. They nodded respectfully as she moved closer, Baker smiling in response to the young lady's characteristically good-tempered expression.

'Forgive us, Miss Croall,' the teacher said in a mollifying tone. 'Simply the idle meanderings of men who should spend more time in appreciation of your father's hospitality, and expend less effort on indolent ponderings.'

Annie laughed gently, though - like the very curator she resembled so closely - she seemed to be watching the reaction of her guests with care and attention. From his limited experience of her presence, Chappelton felt instinctively that she would be good company, though only a fool would underestimate the sharp intellect that was evident in her clear blue eyes. 'You do yourself a disservice, Mr Baker,' she grinned benevolently. 'And you too, Mr Adam, for initially I shared your observation. However, if I may be so bold, I rather think that any suspicion as to the Major's presence may be misplaced. While you are quite correct that an

99

officer of his rank would be somewhat overqualified for such an apparently menial responsibility, the fact - as I perceive it - is that the regiment wish to make a prominent display of the seriousness with which they hold their duty... especially with the local press present, to say nothing of the Provost.'

'In tomorrow's harsh light, on the other hand, I do rather fancy that we shall be fortunate to garner a couple of lance corporals with rusted bayonets,' laughed Baker, keen to lighten the mood.

'Yes, well, be that as it may, I'm not sure that the Major will see the levity in the situation,' Adam reflected insightfully - though not without some degree of humour of his own. 'Attending a social engagement with the cream of the Burgh is one thing - especially when it offers Stirling's finest mulled wine on a cold night like this. But while I do not doubt for a moment that it is a preferable duty to fighting the Zulu nation at Ulundi, somehow I doubt that he found the notion of standing guard over a precious stone to be entirely worthy of his station... nor indeed the kind of merry celebration that he had been anticipating.'

For Chappelton, who had just spent Christmas Day alone in a draughty hotel room, the sentiment was keenly felt indeed. Before he could add his own thoughts to the conversation, however, his attention was drawn to the arrival of Provost Christie in the room, followed at a respectful distance by the curator himself. At the council leader's appearance, there was a short-lived burst of applause. The gentlemen seemed in high spirits, the Provost in particular appearing to enjoy the hospitality on display as he headed straight for Mrs Croall's greatly-admired seed cake with little hesitation.

Noticing her father's return, Annie moved gently away from the group in order to greet him... only to be intercepted in her attempt by none other than Andrew Hutchison, sweeping between the pair like a vulture diving for prey. Although Chappelton had been more than aware of the rector's presence in the room before now, he realised that had involuntarily tuned out the booming voice and posturing bluster from his immediate attention. Now, however, there was no ignoring the wilful headmaster as he strode up to his host with perceptible intent.

'Mr Croall, I must protest!' Hutchison growled, his expression suggesting that he was a gentleman often accustomed to doing little else. 'This is quite unacceptable, sir. Simply beyond the pale!'

Taking a deep breath, the curator painstakingly assumed his most understanding expression before risking the inevitable question: 'Does something seem to be the matter, Mr Hutchison?'

'The matter!' spat the rector, his ire clearly provoked. 'I should say something is *very much* the matter.' He paused momentarily for dramatic effect, drawing himself up to his full height as he continued: 'Sir, being a progressive man by nature, I have no difficulty with ladies being present at public functions such as this. However, I feel certain that I speak for polite society when I tell you that this is no suitable venue for debate by petty dilettantes!'

Emerging from the crowd, her expression more droll than offended, was the sharp-tongued Miss MacLagan. Unlike her mortar-boarded nemesis, however, the formidable archaeologist seemed completely unruffled by the display unfolding before her. 'I rather suspect that I am the one to whom the rector is referring, Mr Croall. Though might I apologise on his behalf for this infantile spectacle.'

Hutchison's eyeballs seemed on the point of bulging from their sockets. 'Mr Croall, I strongly suggest that you exercise more care in the consideration of your guest list the next time you are issuing invitations to such an event. I for one consider it completely inappropriate that I am being spoken to in such a way.'

Croall shook his head in thinly-veiled incomprehension, his gentle voice acquiring the deportment of supreme tact. 'I'm afraid I don't quite understand the problem, sir. Perhaps if you were to explain to me further...'

'The problem,' MacLagan interrupted smoothly, 'is that Mr Hutchison is pathologically incapable of admitting when he is wrong. We were discussing my continued persecution by the Society of Antiquaries, and my decision to donate all of my research papers and findings to the British Museum as a result. They, at least, were willing to consider my contribution to the field in light of my intellectual input rather than my gender.'

Hutchison, still very clearly frustrated at being contradicted - a position which Chappelton had a feeling the rector rarely occupied - was barely keeping his temper in check. 'Being nominated as a lady associate rather than an elected member is hardly persecution, madam. And if I might be so bold, even that eminently sensible decision was a generous one under the circumstances.'

'Mr Hutchison,' Croall interjected, his tenor hardening ever so subtly, 'I think it plain that you have made your point most clearly. However, it is entirely at the Institute's discretion as to which guests should be invited to any given function. While your objections are duly noted, I must tell you...'

'The Institute's discretion? In other words, your own personal choice of guests.' Hutchison glared at Croall resentfully, the tassel of his academic cap bobbing behind him in indignation. 'No good will come of this, sir. It is a scientifically recognised fact that the female brain is unable to process - or even contain - complex scientific or philosophical ideas. The reduced cranial capacity will always make such a concept quite impossible. Is that not so, Dr Schottler?'

Seeming deep in thought, the Prussian academic appeared almost startled by the unexpected enquiry, and turned to the headmaster with a reaction of some surprise. '*Entschuldigen Sie*, sir? I'm afraid human anatomy is not exactly my forte.' His quizzical expression suggested that the doctor was, in fact, questioning Hutchison's own cranial capacity by raising such an issue at a social event in the first place.

'My point, Herr Doktor,' the rector said with exaggerated patience, 'is that women have shown no true aptitude for the sciences precisely because they lack the natural ability to do so.'

Schottler frowned at Hutchison's sweeping statement. 'I am not at all sure that is the truth, sir, if I am to be quite honest. What of the achievements of your Elizabeth Garrett Anderson, or Mary Fairfax Somerville? And indeed, what of the pioneering work of Florence Nightingale?' He paused musingly before adding: 'In fact, if one is also to consider...'

'I grant you that every rule has the odd exception,' Hutchison interrupted swiftly, his voice injected with a disingenuous quality that he presumably considered to be magnanimity. 'However, a general trend remains a general trend, no matter how one tries to obscure the fact. Should your line of reasoning be followed to its logical conclusion, women might even have the vote - and then where would this country be?'

Rather than making her seem disconsolate, the rector's bluster seemed to amuse

MacLagan all the more. 'With respect, sir, might I suggest that you spend less time with your amateur studies of phrenology and expend more efforts paying attention to current affairs. If women are so feeble-minded, might you explain to me why the American President signed a bill into law this very year which will allow female attorneys to argue cases before the United States Supreme Court?'

'Americans!' Hutchison snorted derisively. 'As though that unruly colonial rabble will ever achieve any kind of influence worthy of note. Besides, Miss MacLagan, your protestations are not only socially offensive - they are also deeply at odds with scripture. Reverend Chappelton,' he snapped, turning from his position to address the nearby vicar. 'Correct me if I am wrong, but does not St Paul's First Epistle to the Corinthians specifically indicate the subservient role of women by instructing them to remain silent in church?'

Chappelton flinched, feeling as though he would rather be doing anything other than debating the finer points of theology in such rarefied circumstances. If Hutchison's voice rose any louder, he would be on the verge of causing a scene amongst the other guests - surely the last thing that his host would want, particularly on such an auspicious occasion. Keen to assist in defusing the situation, even if he begrudged being drawn into the argument, the clergyman carefully offered his words in the spirit of the Apostle Barnabus, that great conciliator of old. 'Opinion is divided on the matter, sir. But personally, I would venture that St Paul was offering that guidance specifically to Corinthian women - only in the Corinthian church - at one particular time in history, for a distinct and almost certainly short-lived reason. Though it is interesting that you should choose that particular book of the New Testament, given that it also contains very clear evidence that both genders are regarded as equal in the eyes of the Lord.'

Hutchison grunted antagonistically and, sensing the direction of the headmaster's next tack in the debate, Chappelton smartly appended his statement by adding: 'We should be very wary of applying generalised notions to the Good Book, Mr Hutchison... or, indeed, from using the Bible indiscriminately to advance our own positions on any given matter.'

The vicar's even but pointed words seemed lost on the headmaster, who seemed more concerned with the possibility that he may be losing his own argument. 'Yes, well... my point, if I may put it to you in simple terms, was that women are shown throughout the Bible in subordinate roles for a good reason.'

'Are they indeed?' asked Chappelton, his expression enquiring but the timbre of his voice turning vaguely mordant. 'If that is so, then why would the Lord God - who is infallible, lest we fail to recall - choose a woman to bear the infant Christ?'

'Ah, now, given that to be the case...'

'And then why would He decide that a female should be the initial witness of the resurrected Christ on that first Easter Sunday, a time when women were not even admissible to give testimony in court?'

Hutchison thinned his lips indignantly. 'Frankly, sir, it is my opinion...'

'Furthermore, and several centuries earlier, did not our Lord choose women such as Ruth to serve as Judges over all of Israel?'

The hapless rector, his protestations seemingly thwarted at every turn, looked almost ready to concede the point - unthinkable though the prospect of him ever acknowledging defeat may have appeared to his aggregated opponents in debate. Before he could open his mouth, however, the discussion was curtailed by an unmistakeably youthful voice cutting through the polite conversation that echoed around the gallery.

'Mr Croall! Mr Croall! You have to come quickly, Mr Croall!'

There, standing in the doorway and looking as though he had just run a marathon, was the diminutive form of David Buchan Morris. Though still as dapper as ever, he was out of breath and panting hard, as though he had greatly exerted himself to reach his current position with the utmost haste. Chappelton was surprised to see the young boy present there... and indeed his astonishment appeared to be shared by the rest of the room, which fell into silence at the unambiguous urgency of the unexpected but inescapable voice. Even the carollers trailed off, their rendering of 'Good King Wenceslas' suddenly forgotten in mid-lyric.

'Mr Croall!' thundered the Provost, his expression one of confused indignation. 'What is this... this *child* doing here?'

But the curator seemed as nonplussed as his guests. 'I'm afraid I'm not quite sure, sir,' he muttered distantly, his manner seeming uncharacteristically awkward as he inelegantly adjusted his cravat. He peered down at the newcomer, baffled by the unforeseen turn of events. 'Master Buchan Morris,' he demanded, his now-fearful visage hearkening back to his long-bygone days as a schoolmaster. 'Explain yourself this instant!'

'It was a shadow, Mr Croall! I saw a shadow in the gallery!' Davie was still gasping for breath, his words stumbling out at a rate of knots. 'First the lights went down, and then there was...'

'Nonsense, boy!' boomed Hutchison, somewhat back on form now that the focus had shifted away from his own social *faux-pas*. 'You're talking havers. Some childish fantasy, no doubt. If only I had my tawse with me, you'd be in line for six of the best!'

Croall frowned, still no further forward in explaining Davie's presence. 'I don't understand this,' he muttered to himself. 'The main door was locked after the last guests arrived. How did he manage to gain entry to the building?'

'Because I let him in long before the guests came,' admitted Annie sheepishly as she stepped forward from the throng. 'He has been such a help to you these past months, father, that I promised him that he could be allowed to hear the carollers. He did so want to hear the Christmas songs... but only from the confines of our quarters, of course. That was what we agreed - that he would not disturb the guests.'

Seeming stunned at his daughter's indiscretion, Croall stared at Annie more in disappointment than anger. 'Our quarters, you say? Then what, pray tell, is he doing here in the gallery?'

'I don't know,' said Annie, dropping her head in shame. 'He was supposed to stay in the kitchen. He couldn't hear much through the walls, of course... but it seemed better than nothing.'

'That's just it!' Davie cried, hopping from foot to foot with impatient fervour. 'It was when I was in the kitchen, Mr Croall! That was when I saw it...'

'Not another word!' Hutchison bellowed, looking as though he was on the verge of bodily ejecting the ill-fated youngster through the glass ceiling. 'Your very presence here is affront enough, boy.'

Provost Christie, keen to assert his authority, moved forward into the curator's direct line of sight. 'Mr Croall, this is not acceptable. I must insist that this child is removed at once.'

109

Sighing in regret, Croall turned to his daughter with weary resignation. 'Annie, I must ask you to escort Master Buchan Morris from the building.' Taking a last sorrowful glance at his young assistant, he · added: 'Instruct Mr McLafferty to forbid his readmission for the rest of the evening. His poor parents must be deeply concerned by his absence.' A fleeting but rather sharp look between Miss Croall and her father suggested that more comprehensive words would be exchanged later, in private.

Needing no further persuasion, Annie moved speedily to the gallery door, grabbing Davie's shoulder with a vice-like grip as she bundled him towards the Institute's entrance. He continued to protest, obviously eager to share whatever tale it was that had entered his mind, but Annie's gentle voice could only just be heard tersely warning him that whatever the problem was, it would have to be discussed later.

Preferably, much later.

With the choir still hushed by the unfolding scene, the gathered crowd looked around awkwardly as the gallery's remaining occupants waited for someone to break the uneasy hush. Characteristically, Hutchison was only too happy to step into the breach, rounding on his host with no small amount of conceit.

'The impudence of today's youth! Frankly, sir, I think you encourage these so-called enquiring minds a little too indulgently.'

Croall glanced at the rector witheringly, his abundant patience finally beginning to wear thin. 'It is part of this Institute's remit to support the learning of all disciplines and forms of knowledge, Mr Hutchison. I will not shirk from that responsibility. And, as you may well remember, I was a schoolteacher myself at one time.'

'Hmm,' grumbled the irate headmaster. 'Clearly not at my school, Mr Croall. Within those halls, the word *discipline* still means something.'

'Gentlemen,' Joseph Denovan Adam exclaimed in a pacifying tone. 'Let us not judge Miss Croall too harshly for her empathy towards children. The world could use more compassion of her type, not less. And anyway, Mr Hutchison, I'm sure you too must have committed some youthful indiscretion or another in days gone by; presumably you were not born with that mortar board you wear so proudly.'

'It was only through sheer strength of mind that I came to earn it, Mr Adam. True rigour and self-control always come from within, sir,' the rector muttered darkly. 'Their opposite should not be encouraged, lest it be the rope by which this nation perishes.'

Christian MacLagan was chuckling softly to herself. 'Well, sirs, for what it's worth I welcome the diversion. Enjoyable though this evening has been, I always appreciate a little unexpected entertainment.'

And that was when the gunshots rang out.

111

CHAPTER V
A Murder is Announced

For a very long moment, the gallery was left in complete silence. No-one in the room seemed sure exactly how to react to the two distinct shots which could be heard echoing deep from within the building's walls. There was a long, protracted moment of stillness as the crowd processed the significance of what they had heard; relief that the noise had not emanated from their current position, mixed with the trepidation of then wondering where it had, in fact, originated from. Chappelton felt certain that he had been aware of at least one curtailed scream amongst the mass intake of breath, and suspected that more would have joined the reaction if they were entirely sure of the source of the disturbance that even now seemed to be reverberating around them - or the potential danger that it implied.

The next sounds to be heard, however, were the rapid footsteps of Mr McLafferty as he raced along the Institute's entrance foyer towards the lower museum. Mr Croall, responding in haste as though acting entirely as a matter of instinct, set off in the same direction from the opposite end of the building, cutting through the watercolour gallery at a pace quite unexpected for one of his advancing years. Chappelton, concerned, followed him closely - as did a variety of the other guests. Many, however, chose to remain in the upper gallery, presumably unwilling to risk their safety until the locus of the deafening noise could be ascertained. The vicar could not help himself from reflecting that they were probably the sensible ones.

The curator and his impromptu entourage reached the door leading from the foyer into the lower museum in record time, to find McLafferty rifling at a rate of knots through the contents of a large metal ring of keys which - until recently - had hung from his belt. The sight almost reminded Chappelton of a mediaeval gaoler, a thought that might even have amused him under less serious circumstances.

'I don't understand,' Leonard Baker said, bafflement tingeing his voice as he fingered his starched collar nervously. 'Has the door been locked?'

'For the safety of the emerald,' the Provost explained, 'it was thought most expedient that all entrances to the lower museum be kept locked outwith public opening hours.'

As Annie arrived alongside her father's position, having only just escorted Davie from the building, Mr Croall seemed to be growing impatient with his colleague's inability to find the correct key in order to gain entry. 'Do make haste, Mr McLafferty! There's no knowing what could be...'

'Ah! Found it!' the eager assistant hurriedly proclaimed, brandishing a metal key as he plucked it from the rest of the ring. He wasted no time in jamming it into the keyhole and rotating the cylinder, turning over the lock and throwing open the room's heavy door to reveal...

Darkness.

The entirety of the lower museum had been plunged into a miasma of eldritch shadows, with only the faint glow of the foyer's gas lamps illuminating the outer vestiges of the entryway where the curator and his companions stood. Croall's forehead wrinkled in confusion at the unexpected sight. 'Quickly, fetch some matches,' he impressed upon his baffled assistant. 'We must get some of these lamps relit as soon as we can.'

'Allow me,' offered Joseph Denovan Adam. Digging into his jacket pocket, he hurriedly unearthed a clay pipe and pouch of tobacco (along with some string, a piece of charcoal and what seemed to be a pair of dice) before finally retrieving a box of Lucifer matches. He promptly handed them over to the curator, who immediately struck one of the box's contents against the heel of his shoe and then moved across to light the closest lamp. Within moments, the room was bathed in a dim radiance, its intensity slowly increasing as the flame began to glow more confidently.

The next thing Chappelton heard was Margaret Croall screaming.

All incident thereafter seemed to move breathtakingly abruptly, even as - paradoxically - time itself appeared to stand perfectly still. As light slowly returned to the room, the vicar became aware of several sights all at once. First and most unmistakeable was the prone form of Major Campbell, lying face downward upon the floor of the museum. No blood appeared to be in evidence, though the exposed nape of his neck appeared bruised or abraded somehow, a livid black and blue mark seeming particularly stark against the paleness of his skin. The officer's sidearm lay perhaps three feet away from his right hand, its haphazard position suggesting that it had been thoughtlessly kicked aside by some unseen assailant. The sharp tang of gunpowder still hung in the air from the revolver's recent discharge.

Next to the immobile Major, the room's central display case had been badly damaged, its glass shattered as though from some sharp impact against its front and side. Jagged shards lay irregularly around the case's wooden bench, forming a rugged circle of sparkling debris. But crucially, although the raised container still proudly displayed its velvet cushion within, the Maharajah's Homunculus was nowhere to be seen.

'The emerald!' gasped the Provost, the exclamation seeming redundant even as he made it. 'It has been stolen!'

Taking in every aspect of the spectacle before him, Croall immediately sprang to action with energy more befitting a man twenty years his junior. 'Mr Baker,' he barked with alacrity, 'kindly remove the ladies to the upper gallery and instruct the rest of the guests to remain there until told otherwise. This is no sight fit for the fairer sex. The murderer may still be at large... but, I must stress, say nothing to the others about what you have seen here. We must avoid panic at all costs.'

The art master, his eyes bulging at the full magnitude of his host's implication, obeyed the instruction without delay. Although Annie and Margaret appeared too stunned to offer any objection, Chappelton did note Miss MacLagan's bitter opposition to her removal from the room before - at the Provost's insistence - she eventually assented with grudging reluctance. Meanwhile, Croall was urgently rolling off a string of directions to Mr McLafferty, culminating in a stern command to return to the Institute's main doorway with all due swiftness, and to guard it diligently while the assistant awaited further instructions.

As the departures were taking place, Adam had retrieved his matches from the curator and was hurriedly lighting the rest of the room's lamps. Each emplacement, when fully illuminated, provided further detail to the incident which had befallen the lower museum. Mr Hutchison, with a characteristic eye for detail, was the first to identify two bullet-holes which had freshly appeared in the room since the emerald's unveiling ceremony - presumably the result of the earlier shots. One

116

had only just stopped short of a Stirling Head, mounted high on the wall, as though a shot had either gone wide or otherwise ricocheted without warning. The other was situated just next to the room's large windows, angled slightly above the head-height of a person of average build. Hutchison had promptly suggested to the curator that, due to having some expertise with hunting weapons, he should take custody of Campbell's discarded service revolver, not least to ascertain that only two rounds had indeed been fired from the gun. Croall resisted the notion for the time being, citing the fact that the sidearm would need to be preserved for examination by the police when they came to investigate the crime.

Rather, the Institute's custodian was far more interested in the Major's fate than in the state of his firearm - or even, it seemed, the missing emerald. Now that the room was fully lit, the curator seemed satisfied that the lower museum was empty but for himself and his fellow new arrivals... though from the forensic analysis of the room that Croall's keen eyes were performing, Chappelton felt certain that further revelations would soon be forthcoming. Crouching down to examine the prostrate body, the museum's beleaguered keeper waved across to Dr Schottler by means of respectful summons. 'Herr Doktor, I would require your professional advice - if I may?'

The bookish German scuttled across to Croall's position, hunkering down to meet the curator's gaze over the fallen officer's still form.

'My apologies, Mr Croall, but I am not a physician. I am not at all sure that I can be of much assistance here.'

'Kindly do as Mr Croall instructs you, sir!' Provost Christie asserted adamantly. 'It's your suggestions he has asked for, not a post-mortem examination!'

'Thank you, Provost,' the Smith's custodian nodded, his eyes flicking between Christie and the perplexed academic. But Chappelton noted that Schottler was already gazing at Campbell's fallen body as one might study a crossword puzzle, his hands lightly pressing here and there at certain key areas at the back of the Major's neck and posterior cranium. He tutted to himself, nodding as he made his brisk assessment, before lifting the officer's arm gently and checking his wrist for even the faintest of pulses. A few moments later, he lightly replaced the limb on the ground and returned his eyes to Croall, shaking his head ruefully.

'I am sorry,' he said dolefully. 'There is nothing to be done.' Getting back to his feet, though showing little sign of being shaken, Schottler removed his glasses and momentarily polished them on the edge of his suit jacket. 'I am no expert in human physiognomy, but from my cursory examination I can only conclude that the Major has been struck on the back of the skull by a heavy object - possibly around the area of the pituitary gland.' He traced a broad circle in the air behind the body's neck. 'Whatever it was that hit him, the blow must quite clearly have proven fatal.'

But Hutchison did not seem convinced. 'Far be it from me to bandy words with the scientific fraternity, Dr Schottler, but shouldn't there a more extensive display of bruising in evidence? That area of abrasion appears strangely localised.' Chappelton had to admit that the headmaster had a point; Campbell's body showed surprisingly little sign of disturbance beyond the configuration of its current, undignified final position.

'*Nein*, Mr Hutchison; not necessarily. Much depends on the nature of the murder weapon. More catastrophic signs can manifest themselves immediately, or sometimes much later, depending on the precise site of the impact.' He paused for a moment, pushing his glasses further up the bridge of his nose. 'The cold temperature of the room - you will notice that the fire has died out - and whatever blunt instrument was used to bring about the Major's demise... these are the deciding factors to consider when reflecting upon the nature of the wound.'

Adam cleared his throat pointedly. 'The sad truth of it, gentlemen, is that Major Campbell is regrettably beyond our help. A rather more urgent question, I would postulate, is how he came to meet his end - and how we might avoid befalling the same fate.'

'Of that, there can be no doubt,' agreed Croall, still carefully scrutinising every detail of the room around him as he rose stiffly to his feet. 'After the guests had retired to the upper gallery for refreshments, both doors to this room were locked for the safety of the emerald - the exit to the foyer, and also the annexe to the upper museum. To these doors, only three people had keys. Myself, who was with you all at the buffet. Mr McLafferty, who has barely left his post at the main door all evening. And the Major himself, who was found locked within the room.'

The Provost, who happened to be standing closest to the door leading to the upper museum, moved across and pushed the handle. 'The door is still locked,' he confirmed to the group. 'Whoever did this, they could not have escaped by that method.'

'I should have thought that was obvious, sir,' Hutchison observed dryly. 'There is no exit from the building that way, lest they had then conspired to somehow make their getaway through the lower gallery - in which case Mr McLafferty would have intercepted them - or the top of the upper gallery, which would have meant that everyone would have witnessed their escape.'

'And there could be no departure through the other door either,' Croall mused aloud. 'Leaving through the foyer in plain sight would seem a rather foolhardy strategy for even the most audacious of criminals. Besides, Annie was escorting Master Buchan Morris from the building at the same time that the gunshots were heard, which means that she - as well as

Mr McLafferty - would have observed the assailant's presence in the main corridor.'

Glowering as he racked his brains, Adam noted: 'Then how *did* they escape? The windows are set in fixed panes, and they all remain intact. The doors were locked, the room is quite clearly uninhabited apart from ourselves... so what *has* become of the Homunculus emerald?'

The curator and Dr Schottler exchanged an insightful glance. 'Distasteful though it may seem,' Croall observed delicately, 'I feel that there is one avenue that has remained unchecked.'

'Whatever do you mean?' Provost Christie asked with some degree of apprehension.

Croall gave a nod, and Schottler again returned to a crouching position near the Major. Slowly, the German turned the body over; noticing the trim scholar's struggle with the weight of the larger man, Adam moved across the room to assist him in gently moving Campbell's corpse onto its back, but Schottler waved him away irritably. A few moments later - once the officer had finally been laid into a resting position - it was clear that his face was ashen, its final expression implacable.

Now that the Major's back was against the floor, Schottler gradually and deliberately moved his hands through each of his uniform's pockets one by one, emptying their contents onto the ground alongside the body - always in plain sight of the room's occupants. Hutchison wrinkled his nose in distaste at the morbid scene, though by his silence Chappelton could only conclude that the rector could offer up no alternative to this macabre but eminently logical course of action. Within a few moments, he had amassed a small pile which consisted of a lightly-soiled handkerchief, a notepad and pencil, some loose change, a small bunch of keys, and a set of separate keys which Croall identified as the ones which belonged to the lower museum's two doors.

Of the emerald, however, there remained no sign whatsoever.

His survey of the body's belongings now complete, Schottler rose from the ground, dusted himself down, and without compunction moved across to the side of the fireplace. There, the broad, rough-spun dustsheet which had once covered the emerald's display case was lying draped over a chair, unmoved since its earlier removal during the unveiling ceremony. Grabbing the cover as though it were an oversized blanket, the doctor headed back to the body and respectfully draped it over the Major's prone form, obscuring his lifeless features from view.

'There he must stay,' the Provost intoned, 'at least until the police arrive.' He inclined his head wincingly. 'A sorry state of affairs, this. A man has lost his life, a priceless artefact has been stolen... and for all I know, there could be a major diplomatic incident brewing as a result of this evening's events.'

'If I may?' Schottler requested enquiringly. 'With the greatest of respect, sirs, I would not recommend leaving the body here in the museum. The police, I feel certain, will want to examine it with as little evidence of decay as is possible.'

Adam frowned in confusion. 'It feels colder than an ice-house in here without the fire lit, Doctor. But I admit, a mortuary it most definitely is not. What exactly are you suggesting?'

'Mr Croall,' the academic asked, seeming to ignore the artist's question as he peered over his spectacles. 'Are there any secluded areas of the Institute that we might store the Major until the authorities arrive? Somewhere that is devoid of light?'

The curator looked around the room intently, clearly reluctant to remove the corpse from the crime scene, before grudgingly offering: 'The most logical place that I can suggest is the boiler room. It is dark, secluded... and moving Mr Campbell there might help to prevent further alarm amongst the other guests.'

'This seems like an ill-advised notion, Mr Croall,' Hutchison stated bluntly. 'Surely a boiler room, by its very nature, will have a humid temperature quite unsuitable for the storage of a decaying corp... ahem, I mean to say, quite unsuitable for the purpose that you are suggesting.'

'The interior of the boilers may be hot, sir,' the curator noted witheringly, 'but I can assure you that the room which houses them is not. The system is situated in an area beneath the building - a sort of sub-basement, if you will. And at this time of year, even with the boilers fired up it will feel considerably less temperate than you may imagine.'

The Provost was nodding introspectively in approval. 'You have my authority to remove the body, Mr Croall. I will explain the decision to the police when they arrive.'

'You have my thanks, Provost,' Croall said with sincerity, knowing that Christie had effectively given his guarantee that he would vouch for the action that was about to be taken even if an investigation subsequently came to criticise it. Turning to Adam, he added, 'I would be obliged to you, sir, if you would return to the upper gallery and try to calm the other guests... closing the main door to the foyer as you do so.'

The gregarious artist, though an obliging fellow by nature, was looking deeply doubtful. 'Exactly what do you suggest I should tell them, Mr Croall?'

'You are an inventive man, Mr Adam - your artistry has paid ample testimony to that fact. No doubt you will think of something... but please be quick about it, for the coming act is not to be witnessed by the others.'

'I shall go with him,' the Provost declared gravely. 'Perhaps with a combination of Mr Adam's creative imagination and my influence, we can pour oil over troubled waters.'

Without further consideration, Christie marched from the room, Adam increasing his own pace to keep up with the official's departure. Only when they heard the decisive thud of the lower gallery doors closing, the noise partially muffled by the proximity of the nearby Christmas tree, did Croall turn to Schottler once more.

'We seem to be lacking a stretcher,' the lecturer observed surreptitiously. 'Under the circumstances, with little time for improvisation, I feel that we should simply elevate the Major bodily... if you will lead the way, sir.'

Chappelton stepped up, his expression decisive. 'Allow me to assist you, Doctor,' he said with no small depth of earnestness. 'It seems the least that I can do.'

Croall's eyes widened. '*You*, sir? Surely Mr McLafferty could...'

'Mr McLafferty has his own duties... and as a man of the cloth, I have mine.' Rolling up the sleeves of his jacket, the vicar moved towards the body, coming to rest at the Major's boots. 'We may never know what Mr Campbell's religious beliefs were, or what tradition he belonged to. But the fact remains, I have a duty to pray over his body and commend his soul to the great beyond.'

'A noble sentiment, Reverend,' Croall smiled approvingly, his visage compassionate even in spite of recent events. Or, perhaps, precisely because of them. 'Your good friend William would be proud of you.'

Schottler blinked hard. 'Forgive me if I am being culturally insensitive, but what if the Major was not of the Christian faith?'

'Then I suppose it is fortunate that he is past the point of complaining,' Chappelton responded smartly. 'Even if he did not believe in God, I have trust that God believed in him.'

Their progress into the foyer was slow and awkward; Campbell's bulky mass was spread unevenly, making his body difficult to manoeuvre through the doorway. But with Mr Croall's navigational directions, spoken *sotto voce* to avoid attention, the burdened Schottler and Chappelton eventually reached the Institute's central hallway without encountering any major difficulty. Mr McLafferty, who had not budged from the front doorway, widened his eyes at the strangely unreal scene which was unfolding before him. The jollity of the copious festive decorations bedecking the area only aided in making the whole situation seem even more incongruous.

Reaching into his jacket pocket, the curator produced a bunch of keys and promptly placed one into a door midway along the corridor, sited in the wall opposite the reading room. Swinging the door open, he revealed a dim passage beyond, chill air suddenly intruding upon the ambient warmth of the room's many lamps. 'Through that door, sirs, you will discover a flight of concrete steps. Follow them to the bottom, and you will find yourselves in the main boiler room area. Then, once you have... well, *dealt*... with the Major, please return here to the foyer as quickly as possible so that I can relock the door. Our activities will not remain unseen forever.'

'One moment!' came a supremely indiscreet cry from the farther end of the hallway. Every head turned to see Mr Hutchison emerging from the lower museum, hurrying along the corridor in a manner seemingly oblivious to the need for furtiveness. 'There is something that you have overlooked,' he noted with some disparagement, opening his hands to reveal the Major's revolver wrapped tightly in a silk handkerchief. Placing it gently atop the still-covered body, he added: 'I suggest that you keep it stored along with Mr Campbell; one might suspect that his employers will be glad of its return.'

'Thank you, sir,' Croall articulated modestly, clearly grateful that his momentary oversight had been corrected. Turning on his heel, he hefted the gun briefly as though checking that its makeshift covering had completely enclosed its exterior. He somewhat gingerly returned it to a position of rest atop the Major's chest. Then, needing no further encouragement, Schottler led the way in backing down towards the boiler room; bringing up the rear, Chappelton moved carefully to ensure that he did not shift the Major's weight erratically, a motion which could prove catastrophic during their descent.

The slow progress into the shadows could not fail to remind the vicar of Smith's painting, and the recondite cavern with its unseen secrets forever held so tantalisingly out of sight.

As the two men disappeared down into the darkness, McLafferty moved hurriedly towards the curator's position. 'Whit now, Mr Croall?' he asked curiously, his eyes wide with uncertainty. 'Would ye like me to fetch the constabulary?'

After a very long pause, Croall's countenance hardened. 'No thank you, Mr McLafferty. That will not be necessary.'

'What?!' spluttered Hutchison, his sheer disbelief more than perceptible. 'Surely you cannot be serious, sir! A man has been murdered in cold blood... and one of the largest gemstones of its type in the entire British Empire stolen from right under your nose! If the police won't be allowed to investigate this matter, I ask you, who will?'

'*I* will.' Croall turned to look at the headmaster, his face eerily composed. The sudden glint of steel in his eyes seemed to catch the rector off-guard, if only momentarily. 'Think about the situation, Mr Hutchison, if you will. To exit the building would require leaving through the main doorway... yet no-one has departed since the event began, and no window has been breached. This leads me to the inescapable conclusion that whoever was responsible for this crime *is still within these walls.*'

Hutchison shot him a look of sheer defiance, his expression daring him to deny that his host could not hope to root out the culprit behind the theft, much less apprehend them. Yet somehow - whether from his personal knowledge of Croall's towering reputation, or his inability to find fault with the logic of the contention that had been posited - he could not find the words necessary to counter the wise old custodian's reasoning.

'Mr McLafferty,' the curator continued, his determination growing by the moment. 'Kindly lower the bar on the Institute's door. Until this matter is resolved, no-one will be allowed to leave the Smith - under *any* circumstances.'

CHAPTER VI
Speculation and Accusation

'Mr Croall, this is outrageous!' fumed George Christie. 'I am the Provost of the Burgh of Stirling, and I will come and go as I please. How dare you suggest that we are to be constrained here until this matter is concluded!'

Not for the first time, the Reverend Chappelton found himself somewhat in awe of Alexander Croall's diplomatic skills. Since their group had returned to the upper gallery to reunite with the main body of guests, the curator had managed to harness the room's sense of gestating panic and somehow channelled it into less vexatious ends. First, he had reported the loss of the Maharajah's Homunculus with almost uncanny composure, prudently but painstakingly avoiding any mention of the Major's demise in the process. Then, with immaculate composure, he had informed the gathered visitors that the Institute's main door had been barred until the police could arrive to conduct their investigation. This fact did not sit well with those few among the party who, like the Provost, were all too aware of Major Campbell's unfortunate fate - and knew entirely well that the police were unlikely to appear when they had not even been summoned.

'Please calm yourself, sir,' Croall enunciated soothingly, facing the Provost with implacable composure. 'If there is only one fact that remains crystal clear, it is this: the Homunculus emerald, wherever it may be, has not left the confines of this building. No visitor has departed the Institute since the beginning of this evening's event, according to Mr McLafferty, and a thorough inspection has revealed that all of the windows remain unbroken.' The latter assessment had been made thanks to Leonard Baker and Joseph Denovan Adam who, being among the youngest of the party, had volunteered to traverse the upper museum with lanterns to ensure that the room had not been compromised. They were soon able to report that the capacious area remained untouched and was entirely unoccupied, following which the curator had hastily locked the area back up to avoid any further dispersal of the guests. The reading room, according to the diligent observation of Andrew Hutchison, also remained exactly as it had been left at the beginning of the evening; not so much as a single book had been found out of place.

'I'm not sure that I appreciate your implication, sir,' proclaimed the Dean of Guildry ominously, his green fur-trimmed robes of office appearing deep jade in the flickering light of the room's portable lamps. 'It occurs to me that what you are insinuating is that anyone present in this room could have been responsible for the theft of the emerald.'

Miss MacLagan, peering over her glasses with an expression that bordered on pity, beat the curator to the answer. 'Hardly a likely summation, sir, when each and every one of us was present here in this very room at the time that the shots were fired - a verity to which we can all attest. Whoever was culpable for this crime is clearly operating independently of our party.'

'This McLafferty, then,' Hutchison volunteered with no small degree of verbal gaucherie. 'Can we be entirely sure of his honesty? Not that I wish to cast aspersions on his honour in any way, you understand, but he *was* the only one unaccounted for.'

'Not so!' protested the leader of the choir, a prominent trader from Baker Street. 'Major Campbell was also nowhere to be seen. Perhaps we should consider his story of events.'

Mr Croall did not look amused. 'Gentlemen, please! These random accusations will get us nowhere.' He turned to Hutchison, his facial features unruffled even though his eyes were blazing. 'May I be the first to assure you of Mr McLafferty's absolute honesty, sir. I have worked with the man for the past five years, and would gladly trust him with my life!' Before the rector could muster the obligatory rebuttal, Croall briskly added: 'Furthermore, your accusation makes no sense when you consider the fact that as he is in the Institute's employ, he could easily have stolen the artefact at any time - including a rather more convenient point when it was not being guarded by an armed military officer!'

Chastened and yet clearly still peeved, Hutchison's lips drew closed like the neck of a drawstring bag. To the choir master, Croall offered: 'As regards Major Campbell, he remains indisposed on military business. I am afraid that I can say little more on the matter.'

The Dean scratched his beard speculatively, though Chappelton found it difficult to gauge whether the man was feeling contemplative or simply irate. 'Nonetheless, sir, you must understand our scepticism as to his part in the matter. I was led to believe from honourable members of the Burgh Council that the emerald was to be guarded by two armed servicemen, not simply one. And if he saw fit to discharge a weapon in a room full of priceless artefacts, can we really be expected to believe that he saw nothing of note? That he possesses no observation that could shine a light on the nature of this crime?'

'Come now, sir,' said Adam steadily, ever the mediator. 'You know as well as I do that if our host could offer further details of the matter, he would be doing so without delay. Why, even if Major Campbell were on his way to summon the authorities right at this very moment, there is no further detail on the issue with which he could furnish you.' The nature artist knew painfully well that this was not the case, of course, but Chappelton could tell that

Croall was quietly approving of the steadfast attempts to ward off any risk of widespread alarm.

The room fell into uncomfortable silence once more, and again the vicar wondered exactly what his host was planning. Glancing around the room, he could not fail to notice that nobody had touched the buffet since the incident; clearly even the cornucopia of enticing sweetmeats on display could not tempt any appetite given the seriousness of the unfolding situation. Every face around the room seemed pensive, though for very different reasons. Those who had not been present at the crime scene were naturally curious regarding their host's strange reluctance to divulge his plan of action to resolve the problem; if he really had ascertained that the emerald was still in the building, why was he so reluctant to demand that it be recovered? Similarly, those who did know of Campbell's fortunes - albeit that their words remained carefully constrained in order to shield the others from the murder which had compounded the burglary - clearly could not understand why Croall had not summoned the police at the earliest opportunity. Exactly what *did* this enigmatic curator know... and why did he so stubbornly refuse to share it?

Leonard Baker's brooding expression spoke volumes as to his portentous frame of mind. 'That young boy from earlier - he mentioned something that he had seen. A "shadow in the gallery", or some such. Do you think he may have witnessed events relating to the crime?'

'He is a *child*, Mr Baker,' Hutchison snorted dismissively. 'Always finding menace in their own reflection, and monsters under their bed. Besides, how could he have observed what was going on in the lower museum? By his own confession, he had been sitting in the kitchen of Mr Croall's quarters trying to listen to a distant selection of muffled Christmas carols.'

'The concept is not perhaps as far-fetched as you may think, Rector,' Croall responded meditatively. 'Perhaps you did not notice it during your recent visit to the room, but near the fireplace of the lower museum there is a small observation hatch - around the size of a dumb waiter - which connects it to the kitchen. A useful idea on the part of the architect, for it allows me to keep an eye on the security of the area even from the privacy of my quarters. Doubtless this is why Master Buchan Morris was present there - the singing would have been more audible from that location.'

'Except that he presumably witnessed more than festive music,' Miss MacLagan deliberated aloud. Her face was questioning, as though every sentence was assisting her scientific mind in piecing together a workable explanation for the evening's strange events. 'I don't suppose that he expounded further on his experiences when you were removing him from the premises, Miss Croall?'

Annie, still looking shaken from her earlier experiences, seemed reluctant to talk at first. Swallowing hard, she eventually said: 'He was too small to look over the lip of the hatch, so he was unable to see clearly who was in the room with the Major. However, he told me that he became aware of the lights going out very suddenly, so he got up onto the kitchen table to have a better look... only to see what looked like a shadow moving through the lower museum. Naturally, as any child would, he found the sight frightening and came to call for help.'

The skin around Adam's eyes creased in uncertainty. 'And did he describe it in more detail, this... shadow?'

'I'm afraid he had no chance to do so, sir,' Annie replied in a low voice. 'I had only just escorted him over the front step when the gunshots sounded, after which I followed Mr McLafferty to determine the source of the disorder.'

The Provost rolled his eyes indignantly. 'Really, Mr Croall, is this to be the extent of your investigation into this matter? The second-hand recollections of some wayward child?'

'I have always believed that children are our society's future,' the curator's daughter said with steadfast determination. 'We should not dismiss their views so readily.'

'Annie,' Croall urged warningly. 'This is neither the time nor the place.'

'No, it is not,' agreed Christie with renewed gusto. 'Nor, Mr Croall, is it any fit occasion for you to impede the process of the law by keeping us all cooped up in this confounded gallery!' He glowered heatedly at his inexpressive host. 'A single word from me, sir, and the entire Burgh constabulary would be poring over this Institute with a fine-toothed comb. So give me one reasonable explanation why you have not allowed me to depart this place in order to do so?'

The curator seemed to be on the point of grinding his teeth, so frustrated he had become at the Provost's obstinately authoritarian streak. His voice, however, remained as unflustered as always. 'As I have been trying to explain, Provost, at the moment the emerald remains within the four walls of this building. Logically, I can see nothing that has yet contradicted that fact. If even one person were to depart... well, it goes without saying that the possibility then exists for the crime to be a complete success. Even if the individual leaving the building was not responsible themselves, such a relatively small item could be unwittingly planted on their person in order to be retrieved later. So you will, I trust, understand my reluctance to comply with your wishes.'

The Provost's countenance was turning positively fearful, and Chappelton could have sworn that he could see several of Christie's fellow councilmen on the verge of wincing at the inevitable onslaught that was to come. 'My dear Mr Croall,' he started, the iron projection of civility running through his voice only just taking the edge from his anger. 'I have been the Provost of this town for ten years now, and I have known you for just over half of that tenure. I was not just the man responsible for the opening of this building; in many ways, it would not even exist had it not been for my direct involvement.'

'No-one here would dispute that fact,' the curator said cautiously, 'nor your self-evident dedication to the Institute since its establishment.' For all the carefully-chosen tact of his words, Croall showed no indication of backing down in the face of the council leader's shrill rhetoric.

'Oh, long prior to that,' Christie announced warningly. 'Before ground was even broken, I was the one persuading your much-lauded Thomas Stuart Smith that the town could make use of an art gallery and museum. Lest we forget, sir, that he originally wanted to bequeath his fortune to the Artists' Benevolent Association!' Impossible though it may have seemed, his voice turned even icier then. 'And furthermore, I had no less involvement in your own appointment from Derby... a decision that I may yet live to regret, it seems.'

The Provost's rebuke of his host was abruptly interrupted then by a strange cacophony emanating from the extreme rear of the gallery. Due to the pent-up suspense in the room, everyone was momentarily shaken by the unexpected commotion - an array of

138

muffled animal noises, it seemed, though agitated as though distressed by some kind of sudden disturbance.

'*Lieber Himmel!*' cried Dr Schottler, clearly rattled. Immediately returning from his mother tongue to his usual articulate employment of English, he quickly added: 'Whatever was that?'

Margaret Croall, her nerves already shredded, began to cry. Seeing his daughter's distress, the curator hurriedly made his way across to her, offering a comforting arm as he passed a neatly-folded handkerchief to dry her tears. 'Please do not be alarmed,' he told the room at large, albeit somewhat superfluously. 'The noise you have just heard was nothing more than the sound of my dairy herd. Something must have troubled them.'

'Cows, Mr Croall?' Chappelton asked in confusion. 'In a museum?'

'Not quite *in* the museum, Reverend,' the curator replied, giving Margaret a reassuring squeeze on her shoulder before returning to his previous position at the doorway. 'As part of my contract of employment, the Council have graciously allowed me the right to house a small collection of livestock on the premises for food purposes... cows, chickens, that sort of thing. They are situated at the rear of the building, adjacent to my vegetable patch.'

'And do they usually make such a hullabaloo?' Hutchison demanded, more than a little reproachfully.

Croall seemed lost in reflection, the cogs in his mind clearly turning at prodigious speed. 'Actually no,' he replied eventually. 'Something must have traumatised them. I wonder what?'

'Or *who*,' MacLagan offered with her usual barbed observation. There was little, it seemed, that evaded her notice. 'Perhaps we have been so intently focused on the notion of the emerald being smuggled from the building that we have overlooked another possibility - that someone else may be trying to get their hands on it from the outside.'

'A co-conspirator?' wondered Adam. 'I suppose that may make sense. But how could they possibly gain entry into the building except through the front door?'

The curator was shaking his head intently. 'Quite impossible, my friend. The windows are all accounted for - fixed safely in their frames, as I have mentioned more than once before now. The only way for anyone to gain entrance would be by getting past Mr McLafferty... and this evening in particular, I would not vouch for their chances.'

'Perhaps it would be best for someone to go outside and search the rear of the building,' Dr Schottler suggested. 'Surely we need no further distractions beyond those which have already presented themselves.'

'On no account!' the Provost uttered adamantly. 'There is safety in numbers, sir. I for one would not wish to see anyone's safety put in jeopardy... though, if I might respectfully remind everyone present,' he added, looking pointedly at Croall, 'we are all in potential danger as long as we remain here. A strategy to resolve this situation must be found, and without delay.'

While Christie was speaking, Chappelton could not help but perceive that Mr Hutchison seemed deep in thought. The headmaster appeared unusually preoccupied. After a moment, he snapped his fingers, a look of dawning awareness passing across his face. 'Upon my word, that's it!'

The curator, who looked almost afraid to ask for further elucidation given the rector's previous track record, turned to face Hutchison with a sceptical expression. 'You have something that you wish to add, sir?'

'Quite so, Mr Croall,' the headmaster responded, grabbing his lapels with growing conviction. All he was missing, Chappelton reflected to himself, was a chalkboard to mark down his observations as he spoke. 'Ever since the theft took place, you have repeatedly mentioned the fact that nobody has been allowed to leave this building, thus leading to the conclusion that the emerald still resides within its walls. But let us recall, that need not be entirely true.' The intensity of his gaze grew ever more forceful. 'Your young acquaintance - the boy with the fondness for Christmas carols. He was ejected from the premises before the gunshots were heard.'

'Precisely,' said Adam, seemingly fighting the urge to roll his eyes. 'He left *prior* to the incident taking place. Mr McLafferty and Miss

Croall both witnessed the fact. So, pray tell, how then could he have taken part in the theft?'

'Ah!' Hutchison exclaimed, holding up a finger in exaggerated emphasis. 'But that, sir, is exactly my point. Supposing the act of deception had itself taken place *previous* to the gunshots being fired?'

Miss MacLagan frowned, her patience with the rector's over-thought meanderings clearly wearing thin. 'Consider how threadbare is the logic of your argument, Mr Hutchison. If the emerald had already been stolen, why would Major Campbell have had any reason to fire at all?'

'The boy claimed to have seen something through the observation hatch in the kitchen. But what if an item had been passed through that same hatch in order to be kept in his possession? Naturally not even the most gifted of contortionists could squeeze through the gap... but an emerald, even one so large as the Maharajah's Homunculus, could easily have been smuggled away in such a fashion.'

But Croall was shaking his head intently. 'Out of the question, sir. You are talking about a mere child! Why would a young man of respectable upbringing be considered a suitable accomplice in such a reprehensible scheme?'

'Why, for the same reason that he revealed his presence to us here in the gallery,' said Hutchison, leaning forward with ever-increasing confidence in the validity of his reasoning. 'As a means of diversion. Consider how smoothly his departure was engineered, and also how he managed to contrive an exit through the one doorway available to him. Clearly the boy was the accomplice that we have been seeking - and yet we have let him slip through our fingers.'

The Provost seemed impressed. 'Your powers of deduction cannot be faulted, Mr Hutchison. The questions you raise are compelling indeed.'

'Compelling... but, I am afraid to say, ultimately flawed,' the curator said with quiet assurance.

'I beg your pardon, sir?' Hutchison snapped in irritation. 'No doubt you are naturally eager to exonerate your young friend, but even *you* must recognise the likelihood of his complicity in this matter.'

'I recognise nothing of the sort,' Croall stated patiently. 'Think carefully about your argument for a moment. You say that Master Buchan Morris presented himself here to divert attention from the burglary having taken place, and also to ensure his departure - with the stolen artefact upon his person. But although the windows throughout the public areas of the museum are all set in place, the frames situated in my own quarters are adjustable. The lad is small in stature, and he could have made his escape from there without any one of us even guessing at his presence in the Institute. Even my wife and daughter upstairs would likely have been oblivious to the fact that he had ever been present in our family's quarters.'

'But he *did* leave your quarters - to tell us about the very theft of which he is suspected,' Adam musingly observed. 'And yet I thought that all access to your family's lodgings were barred to the public, Mr Croall?'

'They are, sir,' the custodian nodded. 'To leave the residential area, he would have needed to unlock the door from the inside - which would bring him out into the foyer next to Mr McLafferty, who I have no doubt would have immediately locked it again to keep the area secure.' His mouth tightened tetchily, as though his patience was being tested to its limit by the need for explanation. 'Any entrance to my quarters must be made through that door in the central concourse... and my assistant would have informed us if any attempt had been made to gain access. But my point stands; if Master Buchan Morris had truly intended to leave the building without notice, he would most certainly not have taken the course of action that he did.'

Hutchison grunted antagonistically. 'It is clear to me that it has been many years since you last taught, sir. In times of exhilaration, children rarely weigh their actions logically.' He flexed his hands, as though reaching for a non-existent cane. 'They do what seems to make the most sense at the time, and resolve to live with the consequences later.'

'You do our young friend a grave disservice,' Croall replied, 'not least as your

144

own judgment is at fault here. If, as you suggest, the emerald was passed through the hatch between an unidentified thief and the boy, for what possible reason would there be a delay of several minutes between David taking custody of the stone and Major Campbell firing his gun?'

'Perhaps the accomplice had disguised himself and was not immediately visible,' Baker suggested candidly. 'Or alternatively, the Major could have taken him into custody, interrogating him at gunpoint and only firing his sidearm as a last resort when it became clear that the assailant intended to abscond.'

A frowning Miss MacLagan, however, did not seem remotely convinced. 'The display case was thoroughly smashed, Mr Baker; you saw it as clearly as I did. For the emerald to be removed in such a way would have caused significant upheaval, and Major Campbell - who, lest we forget, was locked in the room with that confounded jewel at the time - could not possibly have avoided witnessing the whole situation. I can see no rational explanation why he would have waited so long before acting.'

'I must confess,' the Provost admitted, 'it is difficult to disagree with your assessment, madam.' He seemed a trifle sheepish now at his earlier concurrence with Hutchison's outlandish theory, but said nothing to this effect.

'In any respect, I cannot fail to acknowledge the nagging sense that we are somehow overlooking a rather more significant point.' Adam was treading the floor fitfully now, his mind clearly racing as he considered all of the possibilities which had been presented. 'Irrespective of whether the boy was involved or not, it is clear that he was not present in the lower museum when the shots were fired. The door was still locked when we arrived afterwards, and the connecting doorway to the upper museum remained secure, having never been opened. So what *did* inspire the Major to fire his gun... and where did his target disappear to?'

But Croall, if anything, seemed even more lost in thought than his artist friend. 'It was not the boy,' he said quietly but firmly. 'Of that, I am certain. Do any of you really think that the Homunculus emerald is the only valuable item to be displayed here at the Smith Institute? The museum holds many rare and significant items all the year round. If Master Buchan Morris had any propensity towards treachery in that regard, his criminality would have presented itself long before now. No,' he stated with mounting assuredness, 'his involvement was not anticipated by the true thief... and, I would wager, his interference would have been far from welcomed.'

'With all due respect, sir,' said Dr Schottler evenly, 'you seem very confident of who is - and is not - involved in this crime. Yet you also appear remarkably reluctant to share the basis of your convictions with the rest of us.'

'Oh, that is your belief, is it?' Croall replied with an arched eyebrow. 'This evening I have been privy to exactly the same evidence as each and every one of you present here. The errant gunshots, the disappearing emerald, the disorder at the rear of the building... and the question over what common factor links all of these different phenomena.' A sly smile began to creep across the curator's face, his expression laced with Delphic ambiguity. 'Well, you need vex yourself no longer, Herr Doktor. For it is my heartfelt belief that I have deduced what has thus far evaded everyone else in the building.

'And what is more, I am now going to tell you exactly what that is.'

CHAPTER VII
The Centre Cannot Hold

It took only a few moments for Alexander Croall to turn his key in the door of the recently relocked lower museum. Determinedly, he had instructed the guests to remain together, to avoid any temptation to drift away from the crowd, and to remain clear of the central crime scene when they entered the room in question. Chappelton found himself admiring the older man's sheer audacity; given that the curator had studiously avoided any mention of Major Campbell's fate, the coming explanation - whatever it might be - would surely involve some logical acrobatics worthy of a Greek philosopher.

When Croall swept through the doorway into the museum itself, he promptly headed for the centre of the room, allowing ample space for his bemused guests to file around the outer confines of the viewing area. Their motion seemed like a surreal parody of the unveiling ceremony mere hours beforehand.

Oddly enough, although the room remained undisturbed from his most recent visit, it felt to Chappelton as though there was a perceptible sense of claustrophobia that he had not noticed before now. The wooden Stirling Heads looked down upon the peculiar display with wordless bewilderment, albeit that their ancient origins no doubt lent at least the possibility that this evening's events were little more than a trifling amusement to them given the sights that they had witnessed throughout the ages.

Although the room seemed brighter now that all of its wall-lamps were fully illuminated, the museum was otherwise unchanged from the earlier drama which had befallen it; jagged shards of glass still lay scattered around the floor, surrounding the central display case with an arc of glittering debris. Of the Major, of course, no trace remained save for the two bullet-holes in the wall; even the faint scent of gunpowder had long since faded.

'My dear guests,' Croall began, his enthusiastic demeanour suggesting that he was about to announce the arrival of supper rather than explaining the nature of a crime. 'You see here the scene of the only theft to have befallen the Smith Institute in its short history... and, in elucidating the means by which it took place, I hope to ensure that it will be the last felony to take place here for a good long while.'

'One can only hope,' muttered Provost Christie acidly.

Continuing as though he had not even heard the remark, Croall swung straight into his explanation. 'Earlier this evening, once you had all been given the opportunity to view the Maharajah's Homunculus at its unveiling, the Provost and I remained behind for a short period to discuss how best its presence may be publicised. The Burgh Council had expended no small amount of effort in securing the loan of that august artefact, after all, and it was our determination to ensure that as many members of the public as possible were afforded the same chance to observe it as you had all been given.'

Mr Hutchison looked sceptical in the extreme. 'A pity that the same fortitude had not been lavished on the security of the aforementioned item in that case, Mr Croall.'

'If you will forgive me, sir,' the curator shot back, 'I will address that very issue in due course.' The sharpness of his glance suggested that he was rapidly reaching the last vestiges of his tolerance regarding the rector's pithy interjections, even though his voice remained mild as cocoa. 'As I was reflecting, Mr Christie and myself stayed on in this room for another reason - to ensure that the emerald was not left unattended at any point. Shortly afterwards we were relieved in that duty by Major Campbell, who had been assigned by the 93rd Highlanders to ensure the item's safekeeping. He was armed and instructed to protect the emerald - with his very life, if necessary.'

'You will pardon my speculation on the matter, Mr Croall,' Christian MacLagan mused, 'but might I ask why only one member of Her Majesty's Armed Forces was tasked with this duty? After all, we have been led to believe that the emerald is of inestimable value. Surely just one supervisory agent - even an officer of such proven military experience as Major Campbell - would not be sufficient to ensure the security of such an artefact.'

Croall nodded astutely, his usually playful eyes now dark and sombre. 'What you say is true, Miss MacLagan. It was indeed the stipulation of the Maharajah's government that the Homunculus emerald must be overseen by at least two armed guards during its stay in Scotland, and the Highlanders had arranged to appoint a rolling schedule of enlisted men to protect the exhibit during its time here. For this evening, however, it was decided that in order to signify how momentous the regiment considered their duty, a ranking officer would be appointed to accompany the emerald during this public preview. In that sense, the Major was acting as the Highlanders' official representative this evening, as well as the emerald's sentinel. Thereafter he was to be relieved by two guardsmen at ten o'clock, ensuring that the jewel was not left with only one protector for any significant length of time.'

'Ten o'clock?' asked Leonard Baker, looking in confusion at a silver pocket watch that he had plucked from his waistcoat pocket. 'But it's just gone a quarter past eleven. Why haven't the soldiers arrived by now?'

Croall smiled opaquely, his unfathomable expression giving nothing away. 'If you will bear with me just a while longer, sir, the answer will be revealed.' Clearing his throat, he moved his position slightly until he was standing exactly where Campbell's body had been found mere hours before. 'As far as the Major was concerned, I must observe that he seemed entirely capable of fulfilling his duties - robust, experienced and eminently aware of the potential for danger to manifest itself in even the least likely of circumstances. Once he had arrived here for duty, I checked that the accessway to the upper museum was secured before locking the door to the foyer behind me. Clearly this meant that, as no further public access to the room would be required until the following day, Major Campbell would be confined here with the emerald awaiting the arrival of the relief troops later in the evening.'

Joseph Denovan Adam was frowning. 'But I'm not sure I understand, sir. The two doors to the room were locked, as you say - many of us witnessed the fact. The windows, fixed in their frames, are intact and undisturbed. So who, exactly, was in the room with the Major - the shadow that Master Buchan Morris saw from the observation hatch over yonder?'

'Ah yes; let us not forget the hatchway to the kitchen.' Croall extended a bony finger towards the wall, indicating the small aperture adjacent to the fireplace. 'As you rightly say, my young assistant - quite unbeknownst to any of us at the time - was listening intently to the action that was unfolding, no doubt with the innocent intention of listening to a little festive music from the galleries.' Chappelton ironically noted that the choir members, naturally still present among the confined guests, were looking rather pale in the light of recent events, and now singularly lacking in the traditional jollity of the season. 'And yet, unseen from his hidden vantage point, Master Buchan Morris was unsuspectingly to have witnessed the jewel thief in action - the very intruder that Major Campbell had been instructed specifically to defend against at any cost.'

Dr Schottler looked so stunned by recent revelations that, judging by his harried countenance, his brain was still reeling in an attempt to catch up. 'And who might that criminal be, Mr Croall?'

'Why, isn't the matter self-explanatory, sir? The felon in this matter was none other than Major Campbell himself.'

The reaction was as immediate as it was vehement. A wave of consternation rippled around the room, fearful glances and hushed speculation mixed with outraged confutation. 'That is the most serious of accusations, sir,' Provost Christie said, his expression hardening. 'I do hope that you intend to provide some evidence to support such an outrageous statement. After all, think of the Major's reputation - the crime of which you are accusing him is punishable by deportation... or a life sentence, at the very least.'

'Perhaps so,' Croall replied evenly. 'Such a crime naturally entails harsh punishment to reflect its seriousness. But the crime of impersonating an officer carries nothing less than the death penalty!'

A further babble of anxious disquiet followed this statement, and thus the curator waited unwearyingly for a few moments before explaining further. 'Many of you here tonight will have heard of the Major's involvement in the Crimean War as a junior officer. Indeed, if you have any experience with the decorations of Her Majesty's Army, you may even have noticed that his uniform displayed more than one medal indicating that he was a veteran of that particular foreign campaign.' Chappelton realised that MacLagan and Adam were both nodding in recognition at Croall's observations - and they were far from alone. 'However, he made one crucial mistake in crafting the fiction of his heroism in combat. Had he mentioned serving at Balaklava, or even Sebastopol, I might well have believed the story that he was weaving, having met a number of combat veterans both here and in previous posts. But for all their gallant service to the Realm during the Crimean conflict, the 93rd Highlanders were not involved at the Battle of Inkerman... and neither, it seems, was our friend Angus Campbell - a counterfeit officer with a fabricated history.'

'This speculation is frankly ludicrous, sir,' Hutchison sputtered, 'to say nothing of being in the very worst of taste. What if he simply transferred from one regiment to another at some earlier point in his career? The Major gave his life to save the emerald that you converse about so glibly, and yet you stand there speaking ill of his intentions - and subjecting his character to the basest of insinuations, what's more!'

At that seismic revelation, the room's low hum of fevered conjecture suddenly fell quiet. The Provost glared at the outspoken headmaster with barely-disguised venom, hardly daring to speculate what might happen if panic were allowed to grip the guests in the current, acutely rarefied circumstances.

'The Major gave his life...?' echoed the Dean of Guildry, until now largely unsuspecting of Campbell's fate. The pallor of his already-pasty complexion had turned positively ashen. 'You mean to say that he did not survive the theft of the emerald?'

'Stranger and stranger,' Dr Schottler uttered portentously. 'Though I fear that all is not as it seems.'

'Did not survive, sir? Why, on the contrary!' Croall responded briskly, keen to regain control of the situation. 'Not only did he endure the theft, but he was never in any real danger from one point of the evening to the other. To put the matter succinctly, the entire situation was carefully engineered from start to finish - with deception as the ultimate goal.'

Margaret Croall, who had never truly ceased to look anything less than shaken since the emerald's theft was discovered, regained enough composure to enquire softly: 'Can it truly be, father? That the Major did not

155

succumb to the machinations of an assailant after all?'

The curator chuckled mellifluously. 'The only unseen criminal here, my dear, was the so-called officer himself. He led us to believe that he had been murdered in an attempt to throw us off the scent of the true scheme which was unfolding. And I must say, but for a few unfortunate errors in his approach he may well have managed it.'

Adam was shaking his head. 'But what of the bruising on the back of Campbell's neck, sir? We all saw obvious signs of an impact.'

'We saw what he wanted us to see, my old friend,' Croall said evenly, shaking his head at the credulity of his younger acquaintance. 'The markings on his body were never examined in any great detail given the tension of the moment... but they, too, must have been a ruse. At first I considered charcoal, but no... that could not be right, given the subtle graduations of the bruise.' He inclined his head, matching Adam's gaze with growing intensity. 'You, as an artist of no small repute, would surely recognise the effect of oil-based pastels upon the skin - such an application, even hastily effected by oneself, may appear very convincing... especially when only viewed fleetingly. And their impression does not rub off as easily as, say, chalk or charcoal. Indeed, as the rear of his neck was only partially exposed, even any potential smudging would be barely visible to the untrained eye. All he would then be required to do was throw that little piece of pastel onto the dying embers of the fire, thus ensuring that the offending item would not be found on his person later, and the illusion would be complete - even if it would not necessarily stand up to close scrutiny for any length of time.'

'Extraordinary!' MacLagan muttered, more out of admiration than shock. 'He had every element of his base trickery planned to perfection.'

The curator's sly smile had not wavered. '*Near* perfection,' he responded archly.

'So there is no body in the boiler room?' Baker asked, the disbelief in his voice almost palpable.

His host was nodding steadfastly. 'Precisely, sir. And that, incidentally, is exactly who was responsible for the murder - *nobody*.'

'But the shadow in the gallery that the boy mentioned...' the Provost wondered aloud. 'What of the strange attacker that he perceived in the darkness?'

Croall turned slightly to regard the shattered display case at the centre of the room. 'The lamps were extinguished by the Major, one by one, to add a degree of authenticity to the attack which was supposed to have befallen him. Finding the body cloaked in shadows would further compound the illusion of foul play. By the time Master Buchan Morris was able to peer through the hatch in the wall, Campbell would already have been moving on to the next phase of his plan.' He indicated the room's large windows, causing the guests to crane their necks as they looked up at the long vertical panes. 'As those of you local to the area will know, Albert Place is supplied with a number of streetlamps, allowing a certain amount of light to filter through the museum windows. A few moments are all that it would have taken to give the officer's eyes the opportunity to adjust to the room's near-darkness. Then, and only then, did he continue his scheme to its subsequent step.'

The curator pressed the forefinger and index finger of his right hand together, simulating the shape of a crude gun. He turned on his heel, angling the muzzle of the imaginary revolver upwards so that the trajectory of its bullet would pass at a diagonal angle through the remnants of the display case. 'The first bullet would have passed through the glass at an awkward angle, shattering much of the exterior but stopping short of smashing the case altogether. This was solely intended as a diversion.' Moving slightly on his heel, he twisted his wrist marginally, realigning the aim of his makeshift firearm so that it was directed more unswervingly at the centre panel of the ruined container. 'Then the second shot - this time specifically intended to break the glass more fully... and, in so doing, to make the emerald accessible to theft.' Sure enough, the flight of the bullet, following the line of Croall's forefinger, directly corresponded to a hole in the far wall which was lodged next to the window.

'Remarkable!' Adam seemed breathless with an appreciation of the sheer audacity of the scheme. His eyes flashed with inquisitiveness in the room's muted lamplight. 'And so the Major was not firing in order to ward off an attack on the display case at all. It was he who was actually responsible for its destruction!'

His old friend Baker stroked his beard in undisguised confusion. 'Do please forgive me if I am overlooking the self-evident, Mr Croall, but what of the emerald itself? We all saw Dr Schottler carefully searching the Major's uniform in plain view, going through each and every pocket. If he hadn't stored it there, then where might Campbell have located it?'

'It is my opinion, sir, that on this particular point the Major again left evidence of his ploy in plain sight... though I would doubt that this would in any way have been his conscious intention.' Croall cast his eyes to the floor, directing his line of sight to the exact point where the fallen Major had lay.

'Of course!' gasped MacLagan, her mouth momentarily slack with realisation. 'The reason why he claimed that he had never joined battle while serving at Inkerman. He said that he had suffered a broken leg and...'

'...A dislocated jaw,' the curator stated flatly, completing both the sentence and the thought. 'He may have been concocting his military service record from thin air, but -

159

whether brought about by a horse's kick or otherwise - I would wager that particular anatomical irregularity was precisely how he was able to conceal a three-inch-high precious stone in a manner which evaded even the most careful of detection.'

Standing in the midst of a sea of startled gasps from the crowd around her, Annie Croall appeared to be stunned by the revelations which were playing out before her. 'So after all that, the Major had the emerald hidden in his *mouth* the whole time?'

'Quite so,' Croall bobbed his head in sober agreement. 'Probably lodged firmly between his tongue and soft palate to avoid choking - an outcome which would rather have given the game away, much to his detriment. And then all he had to do was lie on the ground and await our arrival; face down, of course, so as to divert attention from the fact that he was still taking short, shallow breaths through his nose.'

Hutchison tutted cantankerously, the irritation of his face betraying scepticism at the veracity of his host's story. 'With the greatest of respect, Mr Croall, that line of reasoning is frankly ludicrous. Several of us saw the man lying there on the ground, bold as brass, when the body was discovered. Surely it would have been obvious to one or more of us if he had still been breathing!'

If Croall took exception to the headmaster casting aspersions over his interpretation of events, he showed little sign of it. 'Face down, the Major's position obscured the true nature of his health until Dr Schottler turned him over for an examination... and, even then, a carefully chosen undergarment - a reinforced vest with a small, hardened internal cavity, for instance - would make the movement of his lungs virtually indiscernible to all but the most focused eye. After all, the illusion only needed to persist for a few moments - he could very nearly have held his breath the whole time without giving much outward sign of it. Given the shock of the moment, no such particular observation would likely have been foremost on the mind of anyone present.'

At this, the curator turned directly towards Schottler, his eyes suddenly pinned like arrows to the lecturer's impassive face. 'It does not, however, explain how a scientific expert was able to overlook the fact that a man presumed deceased still had an active pulse, and yet was willing to declare him dead nonetheless.' The meek scholar blanched, the abrupt sharpness of Croall's mode of address seeming to take him aback somewhat. 'There can be only two explanations, Herr Doktor: you are incompetent, or you are complicit... and given the magnitude of your scholarly reputation, the former seems manifestly unlikely. So I ask you, sir: what is the real answer?'

The silence which gripped the lower museum was almost suffocating. Croall's stare remained fixed upon the features of his German visitor, as though daring him to blink first. Every guest remained perfectly still, as though afraid even to exhale.

And then, bizarrely, Schottler laughed.

It was a harsh, guttural sound, pleasant neither to the ear nor to the soul. Yet Chappelton had the feeling that it was malice, not mirth, which was underpinning it. 'Oh, my dear Mr Croall,' the doctor responded, his mouth twisted into a self-satisfied smirk that seemed - until now, at least - greatly out of character. 'Your logic has proven to be beyond impeachment, as always. And yet, sir, it seems to me that you will soon decide that it may have been better for you to have kept such far-reaching deductions to yourself.'

Stepping clear of the gathered guests with unexpected fleetness, Schottler withdrew a gun from the inside pocket of his suit jacket. The quick reaction of Croall's face acknowledged his immediate recognition of the firearm as the same service revolver which had earlier belonged to Major Campbell. Now, however, it was being swept around to cover the position of everyone in the room as the nimble scientist began backing towards the door to the foyer. Chappelton felt it difficult to deny that, rather than appearing desperate at the revelation of his involvement in the theft of the emerald, Schottler's demeanour suggested that it was he who had been left holding all the cards.

CHAPTER VIII
If I Were a Wise Man,
I Would Do My Part

From the wide arc of Ernst Schottler's pistol, it was agonisingly clear to all of the guests congregated in the lower museum that each and every one of them had become a potential target. Chappelton felt certain that he would most likely have heard a yelp of surprise or choked-off scream at the unexpectedness of the doctor's actions, but the accumulated shock of the evening's events appeared to have taken its toll on the Institute's guests; now, it seemed, developments were unfolding so suddenly that no-one had time to react fully to what was going on.

Schottler's beady bespectacled eyes were raking across the room like a searchlight. Still swinging the handgun with the precision of an experienced marksman, his intent could not have been more apparent. 'I have little doubt that the more eagle-eyed amongst you will have observed that the Major made use of only two bullets earlier this evening. That leaves me with a further four, if I am required to call upon them.'

Joseph Denovan Adam's jaw dropped; the betrayal had clearly taken him completely by surprise. 'Ernst, however could you do such a thing?' he asked with genuine astonishment.

'We have maintained a professional correspondence for months!'

'Dr Schottler, I beseech you!' cried the Provost, curtailing Adam's enquiry. Christie was visibly alarmed at this recent turn of events - to say nothing of the German's apparent proficiency with firearms. 'Have some decency in your actions: there are ladies present!'

'Pray be silent, sir,' Schottler snarled, still gradually backing his way towards the door. 'I am not one of your sycophantic public servants... and I will not hesitate to use this if necessary.' He stabbed the gun in the Provost's general direction as though to make his point even plainer.

Watching the exchange with characteristic placidness, Alexander Croall appeared totally unmoved by the clear danger that his errant visitor presented. 'Another careless mistake on your colleague's part,' he observed placidly, almost as though discussing an unfortunate change in the weather. 'That revolver of Campbell's - might I presume that you pocketed it when the "body" was stored in the stygian darkness of the boiler room? Hmm. Another crack in the Major's story, I must inform you. Rather than a typical Beaumont-Adams service revolver, it is clearly an Enfield... a model of gun that I happen to know will not be phased in by the British Army until early next year.' Croall glared at Schottler, as though daring him to disagree. 'Perhaps his time would have been better spent reading the headlines instead of aiming to feature in them.'

'Very impressive, Mr Croall,' the devious lecturer nodded in sardonic approval. 'It seems that living in a garrison town has informed your observational ability beyond the realm of dusty volumes and skeletal remains. But although the model of gun may not be to your satisfaction, I assure you that its basic function is uncannily similar nonetheless.'

The curator smiled coldly. 'Oh, I don't doubt that, Herr Doktor. Not for a moment. Rather, the question that occupies me is what you propose to do now that the true extent of your collusion has been revealed.'

Schottler's eyes widened enquiringly, an expression not without sarcasm. 'An answer that you haven't yet construed, Mr Croall? How very disappointing... especially when you appear to be labouring under the misapprehension that the intent of our plans is known to you in any kind of detail.'

'Your deception has been clear to me for some time, Dr Schottler - if indeed that is your real name. A leading veterinary expert who is unable to recognise the sound of a few alarmed cows?' Croall shook his head in quiet disdain, his bushy whiskers quivering with the motion. 'All the more implausible when it was most likely your own absconding associate who was responsible for causing the commotion in the first place.'

'The blundering jackanapes!' the German spat bitterly, immediately confirming his host's

165

assessment of the situation. 'That was never part of the plan.'

Though Adam appeared reluctant to draw further attention to himself given the circumstances, his natural curiosity eventually won out in the end. 'You mean to say that the Major escaped the Institute? How is that possible, when the main door has been barred ever since the shots were fired?'

'If you ask me,' added Andrew Hutchison, his straight-talking inflection suggesting that he would be offering his view irrespective of anyone's objection, armed or otherwise, 'the real question surrounds how our continental friend there acquired that firearm in the first place.' Seeming almost oblivious to the mortal danger facing him, the headmaster turned his attention to Chappelton, his expression grave. 'Really, Reverend: how could you possibly have overlooked such a glaring detail? You, after all, were the only other person present in the boiler room when the Major was being stored there.'

'I... I...' the vicar stuttered, not having anticipated the line of enquiry. 'Frankly I must protest at your tone, sir. It was pitch black down in the boiler room when we entered - and, might I remind you, I was engaging in prayer during my time there. There would have been any number of opportunities for...'

Croall tutted irritably. 'This is hardly the time or place for crude accusations, Mr Hutchison. Reverend Chappelton's services were called upon at the shortest of notice. He was hardly likely to be conducting a full funeral ceremony down there, with a thurible over his left arm and swinging a maniple, now was he?'

'Gentlemen!' Schottler cried, clearly eager to reassert his authority over the exchange and emphasise the point that his captives were, in fact, still being held at gunpoint. 'While this little debate is no doubt fascinating, I see little reason why I myself must be detained by it. By all means consider yourselves free to examine every aspect of the crime at your leisure... but, for now, I must depart. I have a rendezvous to make, and I have no intention of being late.'

There was a light drone of confused chatter around the room, from which Leonard Baker's voice eventually emerged as the dominant pronouncement when he asked: 'You mean to say that you don't intend to hold us hostage, sir?'

The scholar chuckled to himself, the sound even more objectionable than before. 'Hostages, Mr Baker? Now why would I do a thing like that?' Again, he scanned the room carefully as he took a further step back towards the door. 'I already have what I came for. There is nothing left here for me now, with the exception of the need for an efficient departure.'

With that, and never taking his gaze from the assembled guests, he backed through the doorway into the foyer. The sharp click-clack of his footsteps on the hallway's flagstones could be heard as he made a break for the

Institute's main doorway. With a sharp gesture, Croall signalled his visitors to remain in the lower museum before he, too, strode out onto the Smith's central concourse in pursuit of the intruder.

The sight which met him there was a sobering one indeed. At the end of the reception area, standing next to the revolving door in his customary position, Jimmy McLafferty was staring wide-eyed at the errant doctor. Schottler, holding the gun at arm's length, was pointing his firearm directly at the museum assistant's head, his expression devoid of all empathy. 'I will not ask you again, Mr McLafferty,' the German enounced threateningly. 'You will unbar the main door and allow me to leave, or I will take the key from you by force. Personally, I have no preference.'

The harried staff member's mouth moved wordlessly for a few moments as he tried to process the nature of the dire situation that he found himself in. Eventually, he managed to respond, his voice quiet and wavering. 'I'm sorry, sir. I'm afraid I cannae do as ye ask.'

'Bravo, Mr McLafferty!' Croall barked from his vantage point midway along the corridor, impressed by his colleague's fighting spirit. 'Do nothing that he tells you.'

Schottler fired a fractious glance at the curator, his reserves of patience clearly spent. 'This evening has not been without its qualities of entertainment, Mr Croall. I would respectfully advise that you avoid turning a

168

comedy into a tragedy.' Slowly and deliberately, he turned back to McLafferty, his expression hardening as his forefinger slowly tightened around the trigger. 'You have one last chance to co-operate. Unlock that door now, or suffer the consequences.'

From the soft scuffling behind him, Croall was becoming increasingly aware that some of the guests had covertly entered the foyer behind him. Acutely conscious of the danger, however, they had the good sense to remain at the rear of the corridor, further from the range of Schottler's pistol.

McLafferty was staring down the barrel of the gun, his resolve clearly tested to the limit. He swallowed hard. 'I appreciate yer eagerness to leave,' the assistant said hoarsely. 'But upon my honour, sir, that door willnae budge so long as I've got anything to dae with it.'

Schottler smiled dangerously. 'Very well,' he offered in a low snarl. 'You have proven yourself a loyal employee of this building, sir. Much good may it do you in the hereafter.'

The German pulled back on the trigger.

Never moving from his position, McLafferty closed his eyes tightly, anticipating what was to come.

There was a loud click, almost deafening in the silence of the corridor, as the hammer of the gun struck the chamber.

And then...

Nothing.

Schottler looked stunned as, in that brief instant, he discovered that he had been rendered defenceless. Frantically, he clawed at the gun's spinning chamber, now desperate to ascertain the cause behind the failure of his murderous intentions. Furious at the unanticipated turn of events, he muttered to himself in overt shock. From his expression it was obvious that Mr McLafferty, having been given an unexpected reprieve from the Grim Reaper's grasp, knew that he was no stranger to trauma himself. Blinking hard, he appeared too aghast even to offer a response.

'You are looking for these, might I presume?'

The voice came from several steps behind Croall. The curator turned to see Hutchison sweeping forward in his academic gown. In the rector's outstretched hand were four identical bullets, their cases gleaming like burnished brass in the lamplight of the hallway.

'I took the liberty of removing them before the gun was placed in the boiler room,' Hutchison stated matter-of-factly. 'The reasoning behind my action was quite simple: one should never leave firearms unattended, in case they may fall into the wrong hands.'

'A very wise precaution,' Croall grinned in blatant satisfaction. 'I did notice your diligence first-hand, as I checked the chamber when you handed the pistol to me earlier this evening.' His eyes gleamed mischievously. 'The weight of the gun told me everything I needed to know.'

McLafferty blinked in disbelief. 'Ye mean to say that you knew all along that he couldnae fire that thing, Mr Croall?'

'Absolutely so, Mr McLafferty. After all, at what juncture could the good doctor have inspected the firearm in suitable light without giving himself away?'

The beleaguered assistant exhaled loudly. 'Pardon me for saying so, sir... but the next time, would ye mind giving me a wee bit of prior warning?'

Schottler, who had been standing in the corner with an expression of sheer incredulity, was apparently beginning to notice the redundancy of his previously-threatening stance. Rather self-consciously, he lowered the empty pistol, his eyes flicking back and forth between McLafferty and Croall. Further footsteps could be heard now as a few of the more valiant guests, emboldened by the coolness of the exchange, began to furtively file out of the lower museum to witness the unfolding situation.

'Gentlemen,' said the would-be attacker, clearing his throat in the hope of reasserting his influence over the guests. 'I am willing to negotiate.'

'Negotiate!' laughed Adam, stepping forward into a protective position alongside Croall. 'It seems to me, sir, that you do not parley from a position of strength.'

The German's glare drew daggers at the buoyant artist. 'Do not be so sure, Mr Adam. Please remember that the Homunculus emerald remains in the custody of my associate.'

'Your nerve appals me, sir!' the Provost stated bluntly as he moved into the corridor from the lower museum. 'I will see the full force of the law brought down on you for what has happened here tonight.'

'So be it, Provost.' Schottler, now regaining his icy composure, appeared entirely unmoved by Christie's bluster. 'You may threaten me as you will. Nevertheless, the fact remains that if any of you ever wish to see your little trinket again, I would suggest that we discuss terms.'

'Hmm... terms, you say, Dr Schottler?' Croall was scratching one of his bushy sideburns thoughtfully. 'Very well, then; here are my conditions. You are willingly placed into police custody, where you admit in full your complicity in this evening's events. If you reveal the whereabouts of the Institute's stolen property, perhaps you will be shown some leniency - though I must admit, I could not vouch for such an assurance.'

'And if I refuse...?' enquired the supposed lecturer, his tone sceptical in the extreme.

The curator smiled, the twist of his mouth seeming vaguely diabolical in the foyer's flickering lights. 'Well that's just the thing, Herr Doktor,' he said, almost nonchalantly. 'It seems to me that there isn't really much of an alternative to my proposition... unless you feel willing to offer one, that is.'

Schottler sighed heavily; Chappelton was certain that he could hear the tall man muttering something in German under his breath, and felt sure that whatever the

172

meaning of these utterances may have been, they would not likely have been fit for general public consumption - especially with ladies present. 'Very well, Mr Croall,' he admitted eventually. 'We will play the game your way.'

The lecturer swung the harmless firearm around by its handle, grabbing it by the barrel with his other hand and passing it to McLafferty. The museum assistant blanched, his mental strain still manifest due to his earlier brush with peril. But he nevertheless gave an impression of intense relief to see the gun out of Schottler's reach as he took it - with some suspicion - from the sinister interloper's outreached hand. Brushing himself down indifferently as though preparing for port and stilton, the German turned to Croall with such studied self-confidence that anyone in the foyer would have thought that he, not the curator, was in control of the conversation. 'Here is the bargain I am willing to strike, sir. As you have correctly surmised, the emerald is now long gone - to be frank, I could not hand it over to you even if I wanted to.'

'Very convenient,' mumbled Christian MacLagan, whose meagre trust in the doctor's sincerity had not exactly been enhanced by his recent actions. She appeared to be the latest arrival in the corridor... though, Chappelton could not help but observe, most of the visitors had by now gravitated through from the adjacent room in an attempt to further understand how the situation was being played out.

'No, Fraulein MacLagan,' he said, shaking his head ruefully. 'For me, not so convenient at all. However, might I suggest a strategy which may prove to be to our mutual benefit?'

Croall, himself clearly suspicious of every word to emit from Schottler's mouth, was nodding slowly. 'Go on,' he prompted intently.

Schottler's malign gaze scanned around the room again, ascertaining the positions of those present. He seemed unconsciously eager to maintain a kind of *cordon sanitaire* around his position, remaining outwith the reach of the others, as he returned his eyes to the curator. 'Down in the boiler room, my colleague was instructed to leave me a short note before he departed. In the event that he was captured or incapacitated, he had made provision for the emerald to be transported to a secure location for collection. One reason for my presence here tonight, in fact, was to make sure that I availed myself of that note before I left the building; that way, even if he himself was unable to attend the rendezvous point, I would know precisely where to look.'

'Nonsense!' Adam interjected, his usually jovial expression turning darker with every further convolution offered by Schottler. 'Why wouldn't he simply have agreed the location with you beforehand? Indeed, why should he openly advertise the emerald's position with a note that anyone had the potential to find?'

The doctor glared at him witheringly. 'The note, my dear Joseph, is *encoded*. Using a pre-arranged system, only I can decipher the co-ordinates contained within. But more to the point, he would only have left the details after the theft had been carried out - otherwise, how could he be certain that I would assist him in the operation rather than turning him in to the authorities for a reward if things did not go to plan?'

Miss MacLagan, however, was still far from convinced. 'Oh yes, Doctor? And how, pray tell, can you be assured of *his* loyalty? What guarantee do you have that the emerald isn't already on the black market, thanks to your colleague's efforts, while you are left to deal with the consequences of his actions?'

'Do not think that question has not already crossed my mind, madam,' Schottler shot back angrily. 'Suffice it to say that my European contacts will be required to make the necessary transactions... and without me, my counterpart would find it difficult to get the item out of the country, much less into the hands of a buyer. The emerald may well be famous enough to be recognised as a stolen item with relative ease, but you would be surprised how much the right purchaser would be willing to pay just to know that they owned such a rare artefact - even in the knowledge that they could never share the extent of their acquisition with others.'

'A pity you hadn't chosen the Mona Lisa then,' the Provost grumbled antagonistically. 'No doubt the same principle applies there... and with no disrespect to our friends in Paris, it may have saved our Burgh a great deal of trouble in the process.'

Though Croall was taking mental note of the comments as they were being made, his attention was completely focused on the movements of the eminently unpredictable Schottler. 'And what of this note, Doctor? You intend to trade knowledge of its contents with us in exchange for your freedom - is that it?'

The German shrugged frostily. 'Perhaps.'

'Your reserve of honesty has been in short supply this evening, my friend.' Adam was clearly far from convinced at the legitimacy of Schottler's increasingly peculiar tale. 'What guarantee do we have that the emerald will be where you say it is? Or, for that matter, that you will even interpret the co-ordinates accurately for us?'

'You have no such assurance,' he stated flatly. 'However, it still remains your best - no, your *only* chance of recovering the Maharajah's property. Of course, you are no doubt eager to know what is precluding me from simply slipping away into the shadows, never to be seen again, while I send you in one direction and abscond in another.'

Croall was nodding, slowly and purposely. 'The thought had crossed my mind, sir.'

'And rightly so. What I suggest, then, is that when I give you the details of the emerald's location, you send a member of your party to find and collect it. If they are successful in doing so, then - and only then - I would ask you to set me free to go on my way.'

The Provost was so enraged at the doctor's obfuscation that he seemed barely able to contain his incandescence. 'Oh yes, sir? And what guarantee do *you* have, pray, that we will not simply have you apprehended in any case?'

'A far better one than I could ever provide,' Schottler smirked malevolently. 'For I know you and Mr Croall to be honourable men, sir. If you give your word, you will keep it - especially in the presence of such esteemed company.'

At that, there was an immediate grumble of moral outrage from the assembled throng of visitors. While it was all too obvious that no-one had any particular desire to trust Schottler's account of the situation, every passing moment was potentially taking the emerald one step further from the Institute.

'Very well,' Croall said eventually... and somewhat grudgingly. 'However, I would ask you to remain where you are, Doctor. Mr Baker will take a lantern down to the boiler room and will search for the note on your behalf.' The young art master looked surprised at having been volunteered for this task, but before he could react verbally his host continued: 'When he has retrieved it, he will return it to us here. Then we will hear what you have to say... and judge your words accordingly.'

Schottler nodded sombrely. 'Just so, Mr Croall.' Chappelton's eyes, however, were drawn to the furious expressions of Adam and the Provost, clearly enraged at even the faintest hint that the doctor might succeed in his attempt to talk his way out of his fate, thus sealing his betrayal completely.

Baker, at the curator's suggestion, moved towards the door leading to the back of house antechamber which, in turn, contained the stairway down to the boiler room. The foyer fell into silence as he twisted the handle and, upon realising that it would not move, turned his head to Croall enquiringly. 'It seems that the door is locked, sir.'

The older man tutted irritably at his own oversight, reaching into his pocket to retrieve his jingling bunch of keys. He began swiftly moving through each of the various keys on the metal loop in an attempt to locate the necessary item...

And then, without warning, Schottler struck.

Moving like a bolt of lightning, the nimble German sidestepped McLafferty and Croall, swinging past Baker as he raced along the corridor with studied alacrity. For all his haste, the fluidity of his motion demonstrated an almost balletic quality; his close attention to the positions of his fellow guests had clearly paid dividends. Before anyone could react to the suddenness of his movement, he was standing directly behind Christian MacLagan, his right arm coiled around her neck as tightly as a boa constrictor.

'Alright, that's far enough!' he barked, moving to an open part of the floor next to the Christmas tree at the head of the concourse. 'I warn you all now - one step closer and I will not hesitate to break her neck.'

For a long moment, all that could be heard in the Institute's foyer was the resolute *tick-tick-tick* of the grandfather clock.

To her immense credit, MacLagan did not cry out in alarm or struggle in the doctor's grasp. Rather, the mature and resilient lady stood impassively, as though treating the German's vice-like arm as though it were little more than a fox-fur stole. If anything, her dignified expression spoke less of fear and more of being deeply unimpressed at the sheer crudeness of Schottler's actions.

'Now!' the desperate assailant hollered rancorously. 'Croall, if you have even a shred of common sense I would suggest that you take that ring of keys and get the main door open at your earliest convenience. Everyone else, I would advise against any sudden...'

But before Schottler could complete his sentence, he quickly discovered that although he had considered his movements to be fast, there was someone else in the room who could move even faster.

Andrew Fleming Hutchison, who had been lurking furtively next to the door to the reading room, had thus far been watching the situation in uncharacteristic silence. His profile, in fact, had up until now remained so subtle that the doctor appeared to have overlooked the rector's presence entirely. That was, however, until the infuriated rector twisted on his heel and delivered a devastating right hook - a blow which met the German's jaw with such force that it lifted him clean off his feet. The punch was loosed with such precision that it swept cleanly past Miss MacLagan's head - being considerably shorter in stature than her captor - and sailed into the base of Schottler's chin with implacable accuracy. The hostile action taking him completely unaware, the German plummeted backwards, landing squarely in the branches of the Institute's Christmas tree. Such was the strength of his momentum, the entire tree pitched backwards, its stoneware pot scattering earth across the floor of the foyer as the treacherous doctor and the great evergreen tumbled together to the ground. Hutchison swept a chivalrous arm around MacLagan's waist, allowing her to maintain balance as her nemesis crumpled unconscious in a heap of broken foliage and candle wax from the upturned tree.

'If there is one thing that I will not tolerate,' the headmaster said - more to himself than the room at large - 'it is rudeness directed toward a lady.'

From his portrait on the wall, directly overlooking the fallen tree, Thomas Stuart Smith looked upon the scene with silent approval.

'Dear heaven, Mr Hutchison,' Adam gasped, stunned at the sight of the disarray which lay before him. 'I should never have thought you had it in you.'

'Had you known that you address the varsity boxing champion of my alma mater, sir, you would have expected nothing less,' the headmaster said, puffing out his chest. 'Alas, my days at Edinburgh University may be long since behind me, but I retained more than book learning from my time there... even if, I must confess, this evening I may have strayed from the Marquess of Queensberry rules somewhat.'

Croall, seeming greatly relieved that the immediate danger had passed, took a deep breath before turning to his still-astonished assistant. 'Mr McLafferty,' he said with heartfelt gladness. 'Would you be so kind as to fetch a length of wire from my toolbox? It should be up in the museum. I rather think that we should make sure our guest remains comfortably secure until he can be collected by the constabulary.'

'Gladly, sir,' the institute's junior employee pronounced with quiet reassurance, picking up his pace as he headed around the ruined tree and made his way deeper into the building.

Baker exhaled deeply. 'And the note, Mr Croall? Am I still to retrieve it for the police to examine?'

'Note, Mr Baker? Isn't it manifestly plain that there is no such thing?' Croall said, his tone more jocular than reproachful. 'When the good doctor had Campbell's revolver drawn, he evidently planned to escape with absolutely no intention of retrieving anything from the boiler room. And given the nature of events, he could hardly have returned for it later, could he? The whole thing was clearly a hastily-improvised fabrication in order to buy him some time to devise an escape.'

Looking confused, Adam was shaking his head contritely. 'But you kept him talking in any sense, to help ensure our safety.' To Chappelton's eyes, the artist looked as though he had now reached the very pinnacle of bewilderment. 'So if I might beg your indulgence, sir - and just for the sake of my own curiosity - might I enquire what actually *is* in the boiler room, if there is neither a body nor a note down there?'

Seeming entirely unperturbed by her recent ordeal, MacLagan looked impatient, as though waiting for everyone else to catch up with her. 'Haven't you deduced it yet, Mr Adam? The boiler room contains perhaps the one thing that our friends valued most highly this evening: not the emerald, but an exit from the building.'

'You mean to say...?' Baker frowned intently.

'Of course!' Hutchison gasped, appearing scandalised at his own oversight. 'The boiler room must require a hatch or doorway of some kind for the delivery of coal. Clearly *that* is how our errant Major made his escape.'

Croall was nodding in ill-disguised satisfaction. 'Quite so. As it happens, the coal door to the Institute's boiler room is securely padlocked... though it appears that dealing with such an impediment was a matter of no difficulty to such experienced criminals as

Campbell and Schottler - whatever their true identities may be.'

The Provost was pursing his lips anxiously. 'None of which helps us to explain the whereabouts of the Maharajah's elusive emerald. Let us hope for all our sakes that our doctor friend here can furnish us with some answers when he awakes; nothing less than the reputation of Stirling itself lies upon the artefact's recovery.'

Christie's musings were interrupted by a deafening knock on the Institute's main door. The sound was not simply loud, but positively thunderous - and unmistakeably insistent. Many glances were exchanged around the foyer enquiring as to the source of the noise, but Croall was the first to act upon the disturbance. With Mr McLafferty otherwise occupied, the curator wasted no time in sweeping through the revolving doorway and unbarring the double doors which framed the Smith's entrance. Speedily placing a large metal key in the lock, Croall swung the doors open to provide access to a dozen soldiers, all of them immediately bustling past the curious custodian as they sped their way into the main concourse.

The martial newcomers were followed from a distance by two others. The first was a lofty, rather distinguished-looking man in a sombre tweed suit of a colour which generally tended towards gunmetal grey; he was young, perhaps in his late twenties or early thirties, with a bushy moustache and brown, alert eyes. His

183

companion, moving somewhat sheepishly into the entrance vestibule, was a small boy whose presence had become immediately recognisable to everyone present at the Institute that night.

'Master Davie!' Croall exclaimed in surprise. 'Upon my word, it seems as though you really are a young man who is full of surprises this evening.'

The quick-witted lad looked up at his friend with wide eyes. 'It's a long story, Mr Croall. You see, after I was... um, after I left the Institute earlier, there was...'

'I think perhaps this story might be best told later, Master Buchan Morris,' the moustachioed man said patiently. 'There is business to complete first. Sir, if I may?' he asked, signalling his intention to enter through the revolving door.

'But of course,' Croall nodded, indicating freedom of passage to Davie and the well-dressed stranger before the curator himself joined them in the main foyer area. There, he quickly discovered that three of the soldiers were standing guard over the still-unconscious Dr Schottler, who had now been bound hand and foot - less than daintily, he suspected - by a length of wire obtained by Mr McLafferty. Chappelton felt certain he could detect a certain gleeful satisfaction in the museum assistant's efforts as knot after knot had been added to the German's restraints. The other troops were nowhere to be seen, though their movements could be heard from the reading room as well as further into the building;

clearly they were sweeping the Institute for possible threats, even though - unbeknownst to them - their efforts had come rather too late.

'Ladies and gentlemen,' the tall man in the tweed suit said in a strident voice redolent with the timbre of officialdom. 'My name is James Sword, and I am the Deputy Procurator Fiscal for the Burgh of Stirling. This building is a crime scene, and I must ask you all to remain exactly where you are for the time being. The police have been summoned, and you will each be required to give a statement of what you have observed here this evening.'

Now that the dust was starting to settle over the sheer audaciousness of Schottler's actions, with the newly-arrived soldiers milling around the Institute and the authorities finally acting to resolve the evening's crime, Chappelton found himself observing the faces of those around him. Many of the guests appeared to remain in a state of disbelief, their nerves sorely wracked by the suddenness of the last few moments' exploits. And yet others were reacting in different ways. Miss MacLagan, for instance, showed no sign of having been close to death's door mere moments ago, her expression implacable as though used to the notion of brigands attempting to throttle her on a daily basis. Nudging the rim of his mortar board, Hutchison was mopping his brow with a handkerchief, the spontaneity of his valorous actions having obscured the tangible danger until some moments after the event. And quiet

Margaret Croall, never one to draw attention to herself, stood in the corner silently eyeing the youthful deputy Procurator Fiscal who had made such a dashing first appearance, clearly beguiled by the debonair man's palpable air of charisma.

'Mr Sword,' said the Provost, pacing up to the newcomer. 'I am delighted to see you, sir - though I may say, not a moment too soon. But might I ask, how did you come to know of our predicament?'

Sword smiled deferentially in recognition of George Christie; clearly the two men knew each other via civic duties, though from the formality of their address Chappelton found it difficult to tell the extent of their professional familiarity. 'For truth, Provost, I would not be present at all were it not for the labours of young Master Buchan Morris here. A brave and resourceful boy, sir; Stirling has use of talents such as his.'

The Provost, mindful of his earlier scornful exchange with Davie, elected to say nothing.

'Had it not been for his efforts, the alarm would never have been raised,' Sword continued. 'It turns out that he had been waiting around on the steps of the Institute earlier this evening - hoping to enjoy the last of the Christmas carols apparently, or so he says - when he heard a noise at the side of the building. He went to investigate, and... well, why don't you tell us the rest, Master Buchan Morris?'

'Yes, Mr Sword.' Davie straightened up, almost as though readying himself to give a poetry recital, before turning to address the others with studied concentration. 'After I left the building earlier on, I didn't really want to go home. Well, not right away. I heard all sorts of uproar just as I was leaving the Institute, like a panic, and thought maybe something had gone wrong. So I thought I would stay outside to see if anyone needed help - provided I stayed out of Mr McLafferty's sight, of course. But then I heard a clatter from the side of the Institute and went round to have a look.

'Sure enough, there was a man climbing out of the coal door that leads down to the boiler room. I'd never seen anything like it before.' As Davie became more involved in the action of his story, the pace of his voice quickened with excitement. 'It was hard to make things out in the dark, but it looked to me like it was a soldier. A soldier, trying to break out of the Smith!'

'Enterprising chap,' muttered Hutchison. 'Some of us have been trying to leave for hours!'

Davie continued as though he hadn't even heard the rector's barbed comment. Possibly he was so engrossed in his tale that he was genuinely oblivious. 'Well, Mr McLafferty had barred shut the main doors by then, so I had no way of telling him or Mr Croall what I had seen. I thought maybe it was a burglar or an intruder, or... well, really I don't know what he was, but all that creeping around looked

187

peculiar somehow. So I followed the man in the uniform up the Back Walk for a while until I eventually lost all trace of him at the Valley Cemetery. I couldn't find the soldier amongst all the gravestones up there, you see - there was a mist coming down. But I knew I had to do *something*. I couldn't be certain what to do - I mean, not really - so I went up to the Castle and told the rest of the soldiers about what I'd seen. They didn't believe me at first, you know, but when I explained about the emerald it was different.'

'Emerald?' asked Mr McLafferty, narrowing his eyes in confusion. 'Whit about the emerald, laddie?'

'Rather, sir, the question should in fact be "what emerald?".,' Sword replied crisply on Davie's behalf. 'To be succinct, the regiment at the Castle knew nothing of its existence until Master Buchan Morris explained the situation to them.'

'What?' the Provost exclaimed breathlessly. 'But that's preposterous! Part of the reason for the stone's presence here was in honour and recognition of the Highlanders' military service.'

But Croall, quietly observant as always, had managed to fit together the missing pieces of the puzzle. 'I suspect that on this point you may be mistaken, sir. The Maharajah might well have chosen Stirling as a location for the emerald to be displayed for that particular reason, it is true, but the arrangement was made between His Majesty's court in Patiala

188

and the Burgh Council directly. In other words, the 93rd Highlanders had no explicit involvement in the administration of the loan of the artefact. There is no reason to suspect that they knew anything about it.'

'Ah!' gasped Hutchison in frustration. 'I must be blind, sir! So *that's* the reason why the soldiers never arrived to relieve the Major; nobody at the Castle was remotely aware of the need for sentry duty in the first place.'

Adam's brow creased, the young man clearly intrigued by the breakneck pace of developments. 'But then, if the army was oblivious to the emerald's presence in Stirling, how did Campbell know to be present here? He did claim that his presence was requested, after all. To have maintained the whole pretence in a garrison town without the army knowing about it must have been a monumental undertaking.'

'Especially as the whole event was by invitation only,' added Annie Croall ruminatively. 'Even the guests this evening did not know of the emerald's presence until it was unveiled... by which time they were already here to see it.'

'With the greatest of respect,' said Sword unwearyingly, 'the need to unravel this mystery is precisely why I am here. The Procurator Fiscal's office was contacted this evening by the Highlanders to conduct a full investigation into this incident, as soon as they were made aware of it, and that is exactly what I intend to do. Not only has a serious crime

189

been committed, but an attempt has been made to besmirch the name of one of the country's most decorated military regiments. To this effect, I will be working in partnership with an officer from the Castle, who will be making his own inspection of tonight's events.'

The Provost frowned in confusion. 'Officer? Anyone I should know, Mr Sword?'

'Quite possibly, sir,' the civil servant nodded courteously. 'His name is... ah, in fact I see that he has pre-empted me: here he is now.'

Croall and the Provost turned to see another newcomer entering the foyer, pushing through the revolving door with considerable purpose in his stride. A well-built man of medium height entered the reception area, dressed in an army officer's uniform. The many ribbons on his chest spoke of a distinguished career, the insignia on his epaulettes denoting his rank as that of Major. He had a narrow, sharply featured face, clean shaven and framed by a mane of fair hair which was only just beginning to grey at the temples. He was, perhaps, in either his late thirties or early forties, his air of controlled discipline unmistakeable as he swept up to the main party.

Noting Sword's presence, the newly-arrived officer nodded civilly. 'Good evening to you, gentlemen,' he offered in a clipped, professional manner. 'Might I ask who is in charge of this building?'

Croall stepped forward, watching the newcomer intently. 'My name is Alexander Croall, curator of the Smith Institute. How might I be of assistance?'

The uniformed man was already glancing around the room, taking note of the eclectic mix of guests as his eyes widened at the general pandemonium that had been caused by Schottler's earlier collision with the now-ruined Christmas tree. 'I will require your co-operation, sir, as we aim to get to the root of this strange incident. It seems that there are many questions which require an answer.'

'That may well be the understatement of the decade,' Provost Christie nodded sombrely. 'I can assure you of the support and assistance of everyone present, Major. For that matter, the full resources of the Burgh of Stirling will be at your disposal - the perpetrators of this outrage must be brought to justice.'

'May I echo the Provost's sentiment entirely,' Croall concurred readily. 'Though if I may say, sir, you appear to have me at a disadvantage. I always value the opportunity to work with Her Majesty's Armed Forces wherever appropriate, but in all my dealings with the Castle I don't believe that we have had occasion to meet.'

'Forgive me for not introducing myself,' the officer said brusquely, the urgency of his duties affording him little time for niceties. 'I have only recently returned to the Castle from an overseas tour of duty, which may well be the reason why we have not yet been acquainted.

'I am Major Angus Campbell, of the 93rd Highland Regiment - at your service, sir.'

EPILOGUE
They Also Serve Who
Stand and Wait

The crisp frost of that cold Tuesday morning reminded the Reverend Chappelton of his first visit to the Smith Institute only a mere handful of days beforehand. Even now it seemed like an eternity, an age lost to the past... though given the events that he had witnessed during his time in Stirling, it seemed safe to say that he was in little danger of forgetting the museum or its unflappable curator at any time in the near future.

There seemed to be few remaining vestiges of the late weekend snowfall in the Institute's grounds as the vicar made his way up the wide pathway once more. How very still the atmosphere seemed in comparison to the fraught experiences of the previous Saturday night. The gentle chirp of birdsong could be heard from the trees and occasional hedge bordering the iron railings which marked the building's perimeter, the cheerfulness of the sound this chilly winter's day reminding Chappelton that in spite of everything, life still soldiered on.

He almost felt reluctant to leave the quiet idyll of the Smith's gardens too soon, so much was he enjoying the air of calm which permeated the atmosphere there. The young cleric had, in fact, been in the process of packing his luggage in order to leave Stirling when the receptionist at the Waverley Temperance had knocked at the door of his room, informing him that a note had been left at the hotel's front desk for his attention. Mr Croall, it seemed, had requested the pleasure of Chappelton's company one final time before his departure. The appeal had surprised the clergyman, who until that point had assumed that the curator must have had his work cut out following the tumultuous outcome from their last meeting at the Institute. It would, however, have seemed impolite in the extreme to ignore the invitation of his erstwhile host - particularly given Croall's exceptional kindness towards him during his visit to the town.

Mr McLafferty, present as ever in close proximity to the building's revolving door, seemed delighted to see Chappelton upon his arrival, greeting the vicar as though the gaunt Englishman was a long-lost friend. Clearly, it seemed to the parson, the fraught events surrounding the visiting exhibition of December 1879 had made companions of them all, forging a common bond that would likely never have existed save for the perils of that fateful night. The jocular museum assistant genially informed Chappelton that the curator was waiting for him in the reading room, hastily ushering him along the corridor towards the doorway. The vicar noted with no small surprise that the Institute's Christmas tree had been removed from the premises long before the Twelfth Night; no evidence of its presence now remained at the end of the entrance foyer - not even an errant drop of candle wax.

The untroubled ambience of the reading room seemed markedly different to that of his previous visit. The plaster replicas of the Stirling Heads remained, of course, very much in evidence on the ceiling, seeming to stare down on the curate's position with a mixture of curiosity and detached disdain. The general atmosphere of the room, however, was greatly changed. Although the coal fire still flickered cosily, its flames continuing to bathe the spines of the library's varied rows of books in a warm glow even in the mid-morning sunlight, the area was now devoid of the chattering guests who had occupied so much of the room at the exhibition event. Instead, the reading room was thinly populated by a relatively small number of seated gentlemen, their features obscured by the rustling pages of broadsheet newspapers. Conversation was clearly discouraged here, albeit politely, for Chappelton observed that no two of the room's occupants were sitting particularly close to each other, as though eager to persuade against the very possibility of discussion.

It did not surprise the parson too much, then, to note that one of the readers was none other than the curator himself. Hearing the sound of the door being opened, the ever-inquisitive Alexander Croall had immediately put his copy of the *Glasgow Herald* down upon the seat of his leather chair and hopped to his feet, marching across to meet his newly-arrived visitor. 'My dear Mr Chappelton!' he exclaimed cordially, as though greeting one of his oldest acquaintances. The vicar noted that Croall seemed considerably more comfortable back in his curatorial attire; the bulging pockets of his frock coat seemed even more capacious than had been the case on their first encounter, leading Chappelton to wonder whether the entire contents of Pandora's Box were stored away in the furthest recesses of that commodious garment. 'I am delighted to see that you are able to join me here,' the curator continued with sincerity. 'If I am entirely honest, I did wonder whether I would be able to reach you in time.'

'In truth, sir, you almost did not,' Chappelton said, smiling at the warmth of Croall's generous hospitality. Like his host, he kept his voice deliberately low so as to avoid disturbing the room's readers overduly. 'I was very nearly packed and ready to go, as it happens. I considered the fact that if I departed today, I would be back home to my parish in Whinmoor in time for New Year's Eve - surely an appropriate time to embrace new beginnings, if ever there was one.'

'Quite so,' Croall agreed, nodding sagaciously. 'And I have little doubt that you will have much to regale your parishioners with, when they hear your account of the excitement here a few days ago. Enough material for a few sermons, I shouldn't wonder.

Ah, but where are my manners? Please, come and join me.'

With a subtle gesture of his arm, the curator invited Chappelton over to a seat by the fire, where they could converse further in comfort. As Croall was easing himself back into his chair, the vicar enquired politely: 'There is certainly no doubt that an evening at the Smith Institute leaves a lasting impression, Mr Croall. But I must risk predictability by asking: have any further developments been made with regard to the investigation into the missing emerald?'

Croall blew air from his cheeks, as though unsure where even to begin. 'Developments, sir? How does one thread a needle when blindfolded?'

'Slowly and carefully?' suggested Chappelton.

'And in that endeavour, as in this one, patience is not only a virtue... it is the very instrument by which we might prevail. Yesterday I spoke with a member of the local constabulary, a senior officer who has been involved in the interrogation of our friend Ernst Schottler. It may not surprise you to know that the doctor is not at all who - or what - he seems to be.'

The vicar raised an eyebrow in polite uncertainty. 'Are you suggesting that he is not a Prussian citizen, sir?'

Croall's lip curled wryly. 'Oddly enough, that seems to be the only aspect of his identity that *is* authentic. His real name is Karlheinz

Engelmann, and he is a highly accomplished thief of rare artefacts... who, I might add, is currently wanted by the *Nuremburgen Polizei* in connection with a number of stolen paintings taken from a municipal art gallery. This has come as no small surprise to the *real* Dr Ernst Schottler, who of course never left the confines of the University of Heidelberg and thus remained totally oblivious to what happened here until news of the crime eventually reached his office.'

'Good gracious,' muttered the curate. 'So there really *was* a Dr Schottler? A veterinary scholar who had corresponded with Joseph Denovan Adam about animal biology?'

'But of course,' Croall agreed, 'or how else would the impostor's presence at the Institute have seemed plausible? The subterfuge had to be absolutely watertight. Mr Adam had been in touch with the doctor - the real one - quite regularly on points of anatomical interest, until the time came to make the arrangements for his visit to the Craigmill Studio. At that juncture, it appears that the mail had been intercepted in transit, and a forged response sent back in order to agree to Schottler's presence here in Scotland. Joseph had no idea what the real Schottler actually looked like, you see, having never seen a likeness of the man. And so Engelmann simply insinuated himself into the role, hoping that his skills of improvisation would hold out long enough for him to inveigle his way into being present here on the night of the burglary.'

Chappelton blinked hard, now quite obviously confused. 'I'm not sure I understand, sir. Nobody knew about the emerald's presence here at the Institute, save for yourself and Provost Christie. So how would this Engelmann have been able to plan in advance for its theft?'

The curator's mouth pursed, his expression turning strangely Sphinx-like. 'I will explain the matter fully in time, of course. But as far as that charlatan is concerned, the authorities on the continent are working closely with our own police force - very closely, as it happens, for in their last telegram they have expressed a clear interest in interviewing Herr Engelmann themselves at the earliest opportunity.'

'Thank heaven for modern communications,' Chappelton said abstractedly. 'Presumably his observation about selling the emerald on the black market was also true, then?'

'It seems the most probable answer. Certainly the police have left no stone unturned in disseminating news of the incident to the general public, in the hope of apprehending the thief responsible. Mr Sword has been determined to get to the bottom of the matter. Actually,' the curator noted conspiratorially, 'he seemed quite taken with the Institute during his time in the building. Perhaps he will choose to visit us again in the future, where I hope he will spend time here in more favourable circumstances.'

'And the emerald itself?' asked the vicar ponderingly. 'Have there been any sightings of it since the theft?'

Croall looked increasingly reflective. 'The *Stirling Observer* reporter published a particularly thorough account of events, of course. Considering that he had only been assigned to convey the details of a visiting exhibition, after all, I rather suspect that the resulting events were considerably more than the poor man had bargained for. Now the whole Burgh will know of the selfless bravery of Andrew Fleming Hutchison, the stoicism of Christian MacLagan, and the resourcefulness of a certain young David Buchan Morris. But before any leads from members of the public could be followed up, something else was brought to light which rather changed the playing field somewhat.'

The curator reached around the side of his chair and retrieved the newspaper that he had displaced in order to sit down. He smoothed it with one hand and passed it to Chappelton. The vicar peered over his spectacles at the front page headline: 'DISASTER AT TAY BRIDGE: Ninety Souls Feared Lost in Railway Tragedy'.

'No doubt you will have heard the news by now,' Croall said grimly. 'Some two days ago, the collapse of the Bridge of Tay as a result of hurricane-force winds. A passenger train was lost that night, along with most of the bridge's high girders. No survivors have been recovered... indeed, none are expected to be.'

Ever more perplexed, Chappelton returned his gaze from the newspaper to his muted host. 'A terrible calamity, sir: there is no question about it. And to think that Her Majesty traversed the very same bridge earlier this year!' The clergyman shuddered, as though there was ice in his veins. 'May God have mercy on the lives of those who perished in those icy waters last Sunday night; at least the outcome would have been swift. But without wishing to seem indelicate, sir, I fail to understand how it relates to the theft of the Maharajah's Homunculus.'

'Like I said, the police were very thorough in investigating every avenue of the theft,' the Institute's custodian noted, unruffled but intent. 'They followed the footsteps that Davie took along the Back Walk in pursuit of the bogus Major Campbell, and discovered a carpet bag hidden away in the farther reaches of the Valley Cemetery. In it, they found a Major's dress uniform - complete with medals - and several other items, including a false beard and a wig. Clearly he had stored the bag there ahead of time, in order to have a change of clothes to hand once he had made his escape - a ruse which, upon leaving the Institute, he promptly used to its full benefit. His appearance now greatly altered, all he had to do was keep a low profile until the following day in order to evade suspicion, before eventually making an attempt to leave Stirling so that he could rejoin with Engelmann at their prearranged rendezvous point.'

Chappelton felt his jaw slacken as the story's inevitable conclusion loomed into view. 'So he made his getaway by rail...?'

'I'm afraid so,' Croall replied, not entirely without sympathy. 'When common assumption may have been that he would have travelled to the more densely-populated south to meet his scheduled rendezvous point - thus seeking to lose himself in a crowd, so to speak - he actually headed for Edinburgh and, from there, boarded the North British Railway train to Aberdeen via Dundee on Sunday evening. Perhaps he intended to board a ship bound for the continent; it is likely that we may never know. Whatever his plans were, he clearly could not have anticipated the storm which was to affect the whole country that night... or, for that matter, that the Tay Bridge was to give way during his journey. Now we have been robbed of the chance to hear his account of events - even his name remains an enigma, as Engelmann claims that his associate always made use of an alias.'

'But if he travelled incognito, how can you be sure that he was on the train affected by this catastrophe? I assume that Engelmann could not be aware of his colleague's fate, if he was in police custody at the time of the disaster.'

'Oh, I have significantly more compelling proof than that,' the curator smiled mirthlessly, his characteristic good humour strangely muted. 'Mr Kidston!' he said, raising his voice as he turned slightly in his chair. 'I wonder if you might join us for a moment, if you please.'

On the far side of the room, hunched between two windows situated to the front of the building and an impressively-stocked case of leatherbound books, a youthful man was in the process of browsing the volumes in search of some as-yet-unfound tome. He could only have been in his late twenties, by Chappelton's reckoning, and yet he had an intellectual, academic air which somehow managed to make him seem considerably older than his years. Though he was dressed smartly, there was something about the way that his clothes hung haphazardly on his gangly frame that made him appear slightly dishevelled. His sharp features and hooked nose were framed by a shock of wild brown hair. The eccentric-looking gentleman wasted no time in making his way across to the fireplace, where he nodded in polite acknowledgement to Chappelton before addressing his host. 'Alexander,' he said, his voice slightly reedy. 'Thank you again for your recommendations; the work of Waldemar Christofer Brøgger has made for particularly fascinating reading.'

'The Reverend Mr Chappelton,' Croall said by way of introduction, 'might I present Mr Robert Kidston: a regular visitor here to the Smith Institute, and Joint Secretary of the Stirling Horticultural and Natural History Society. It seems almost superfluous to add, he is a mineralogist and palaeobotanist of no small distinction.'

'Our mutual friend flatters me, sir,' Kidston intoned modestly to the vicar. 'Though it must be said, when one lives more or less across the street from a well-stocked establishment such as this one, the temptation to regularly peruse the shelves may at times prove overwhelming.'

'A pleasure, Mr Kidston, I'm sure,' Chappelton smiled thinly, wondering what purpose Croall had in mind by summoning the young man to his side.

The curator turned to his young acquaintance. 'I apologise for interrupting your reading, Robert, but I must ask... have you confirmed it?'

Kidston grinned eagerly, his enthusiasm almost infectious. 'Indeed I have, my friend. And what's more, there is little doubt in my mind that the findings have proven conclusive.' He reached inside his jacket and plucked a small object from an inside pocket. Gingerly, he produced a small piece of white cloth which resembled nothing less than a large cotton handkerchief. Unwrapping it delicately, the young scientist pulled an item from the heart of the material which he handed over to Croall without compunction.

The vicar found himself quite literally lost for words. There, in the curator's hands, was the Maharajah's Homunculus.

'Is... is that...?' Chappelton stammered, astonished at the emerald's presence.

'If you are asking whether it matches the item taken from the Institute on Saturday night, sir, then the answer is most definitely yes.' Kidston seemed like an affable enough character, but there was no doubting that when it came to science, he was all business. 'It was found hidden upon the person of one of the bodies recovered from the aftermath of the Tay Bridge Disaster. In fact, when one thinks about it in strictly statistical terms, it is nothing short of a miracle that it was discovered at all given its size; clearly its temporary owner went to some length in order to keep it safe.'

'Only a pity that he could not have done the same for himself,' Croall mused sadly as he gazed at the multifaceted stone. 'With all of his resourcefulness and ingenuity, it seems such a waste that he had declined to commit himself to something other than a life of crime.'

'Yes,' Kidston nodded. 'And, in the end, all for nothing. If only he had known that he was sacrificing his life for a forgery.'

There was a moment of such profound silence during that particular juncture that, on retrospect, Chappelton felt sure he could have heard a dog barking in Edinburgh.

'A forgery, sir? You mean to say that...?'

'Yes indeed! And really quite clever, don't you think?' the young mineralogist beamed earnestly. 'When Alexander asked me to create an exact duplicate of the real Homunculus, I found myself racking my brains; what substance could I call upon to simulate the appearance and weight of an emerald of such international acclaim? After all, with no original artefact to work from, I found myself forced to crib my knowledge from third-hand accounts and documentary evidence. In the end I had to rely on a form of coloured glass, with a few additions here and there to ensure its viscosity, and its reflective characteristics were... well, I won't bore you with the specifics, sir. I am just grateful that my efforts were not in vain.'

Now completely mystified, Chappelton scratched his neck around the confines of his dog collar in bewilderment before asking the unavoidable question: 'So if this emerald is a forgery - and, indeed, it was the very same item which was stolen from the display case in the museum during the exhibition event - what, might I ask, happened to the original?'

Croall seemed quietly amused at the younger man's puzzlement. 'The real emerald, sir? Why, by now I should imagine that it is safely back at the Maharajah of Patiala's palace in Punjab Province.'

The vicar shook his head, still none the wiser. 'So it was never actually present in Stirling in the first place, then?'

'No, sir. At least, not for any longer than a few moments. Suffice it to say that when I became aware that the artefact's safety was in jeopardy, I ensured that it was returned to its owner as soon as possible in order to remove it from risk - prior to the unveiling ceremony taking place, of course. Rather than being offended, the Maharajah was apparently quite appreciative of our candour in the matter. His

Highness had no more desire to see his property put in jeopardy than we did.'

'I do apologise, Mr Croall,' Chappelton admitted bluntly, 'but I'm afraid I cannot comprehend your version of events. You say that you were aware that the emerald was at risk from theft, and yet you have also pointed out that on the night of the burglary only you and the Provost knew that the stone was present at the Institute for the anniversary event. So how could you possibly have suspected that the prospect of the crime was likely - or even possible, for that matter?'

The curator sighed patiently, as though anticipating an uphill struggle. 'According to the police, the emerald's theft was made possible because of intercepted mail which gave the criminals all the information they needed to plan their felonious actions. In the case of Engelmann, as I mentioned earlier, postal deliveries were interrupted between the Craigmill Studio and the University of Heidelberg in order to insinuate an intruder into Joseph Denovan Adam's confidence - under the guise of the respected Dr Schottler. For the ersatz Major, official correspondence between myself and Stirling Castle was seized in order for the impostor to attend the event while the 93rd Highlanders were completely unaware of the emerald's presence - which, I might add, was always supposed to be a secret until the night of the unveiling in any case, and to that effect was treated with the utmost regard to confidentiality.'

'Surely that explains how they obtained their invitations,' the cleric wondered aloud. 'But it still offers no account of how the criminals knew that the Maharajah's Homunculus would be present here in order to make preparations for stealing it.'

'No, sir, it does not.' Croall's expression was growing more inscrutable by the moment. 'After all, the negotiations between the Provost's office and the Maharajah's court in Patiala were largely conducted by telegram, and so far as we can tell there was no interception of communications via that method. Rather, the information must have been disclosed by other methods; indeed, by somewhat more insidious means.'

'How might that be, sir?' Chappelton asked. 'Their investigative skills must have been second to none. After all, if I were an international jewel thief or a master of disguise, I can only imagine that I would want to ensure that my activities were unimpeded by any possibility of error, in order to avoid exactly the fate that they have suffered.'

'Very true, sir,' the curator said pointedly. 'But then, it seems to me that you have committed a substantial error of your own, because you have convinced me without doubt that you are not the Reverend Sebastian Chappelton.'

A very long moment passed then, so much so that Kidston began glancing between the two men as though guessing which would blink first.

'I beg your pardon, sir?' Chappelton asked carefully. 'If this is some kind of attempt at humour, I find it in very poor taste.'

Croall tutted loudly, shaking his head in firm conviction. 'Oh, come now. A vicar who was unable to tell the difference between a maniple and a thurible? Even a layman would know that a metal censer and a piece of clerical attire are not even remotely alike... and yet you said nothing. Why should that be?'

'Upon my word,' the clergyman spluttered, his face reddening. 'Do you not recall the circumstances in which you raised that subject? In what manner would it have been appropriate for me to correct you on a point of obscure ecclesiastical minutiae when we believed our very lives to be in peril?'

'Perhaps you're right,' Croall conceded meekly... before carrying on regardless. 'However, I also became mistrustful of your identity when you didn't recognise my daughter Mary's name, even though you had claimed to be one of my son's closest acquaintances. Young Mary is his favourite sister, you see, and it seemed unusual that he would not have spoken of her to a confidante... but I admit, that fact alone proved nothing.

'Then, however, I learned from Mr Hutchison that you had not recognised the name of the Drummond Tract Depot - a company which, while local to Stirling, is known to clergymen across the globe for its Christian publications. Your lack of awareness surrounding that fact may have riled him for its anti-intellectual connotations, but it provoked my own suspicions for entirely different reasons: what parson would not have even a vague recollection of the Drummond company's output? After all, in its time it has published everything from theological texts to Sunday school prizes.'

Chappelton's expression grew conflicted, as though he seemed unsure whether to panic or simply become indignant at the connotations of the curator's argument. 'Mr Croall, with the greatest of respect, need I remind you that I am still mourning the sudden death of a loved one? Whilst I am hugely indebted to you for your kind hospitality during my stay here, I must protest at the insinuations that you are making. Is it not enough that you have recovered your stolen artefact, falsified though it may be, without finding perils hidden in your own shadow?'

Croall's reply was to reach into the breast pocket of his frock coat and pull out a small, folded piece of paper. Gently, he opened it up, though its contents remained obscured to Chappelton's vision. 'This is a telegram which I received from my son on Christmas Day,' the curator explained matter-of-factly. 'I had wired him a similar communication on Christmas Eve, explaining that his good friend had arrived safely in Stirling. I was curious as to why he hadn't told me to expect your presence here, and in spite of the expense a telegram seemed faster than a letter - especially at this time of year.

'I was keen to know more about the Reverend Mr Chappelton. What sort of interests did he enjoy, for instance? What kind of subjects may fascinate his intellect - and more to the point, what could I do to make him feel at home at a time of considerable emotional distress? After all, he would be spending Christmas alone amongst strangers.

'Imagine my surprise, then, when I should receive this communication from William the very next day, informing me of his confusion with regard to my account of events. I should, in fact, have considered myself fortunate to hear from him at all, given that after the morning service in celebration of the Nativity, he was due to be a Christmas dinner guest at Whinmoor Parish.

'A festive meal which was to be hosted by the Reverend Sebastian Chappelton... and his wife Gwendolyn.'

The vicar said nothing.

'I say!' Kidston exclaimed enthusiastically, as though he had been invited to an amateur dramatics display. 'This is most exciting.'

But Croall was in no mood for his narrative to be interrupted in mid-flow. 'It occurred to me then that I had contacted William about the emerald earlier in the month - albeit in the strictest confidence, as no-one outside of the Provost's inner circle was even remotely aware that it was to be loaned by the Maharajah. Given his geographical distance, it seemed safe to convey news to him of the surprise that we were intending to bring to Stirling. But lo and behold, the telegram made it clear that my son never received that letter. It had simply vanished, as though lost in the post... except that it didn't go astray at all, did it?' His gaze grew in indignant fervour. 'It was simply purloined by an unscrupulous mountebank who was willing to impersonate a grieving man of God so that he could mastermind the perfect crime - or so you thought, no doubt.'

For a long moment, it seemed as though the reading room - indeed, even the world around it - was standing still.

'You can prove nothing,' Chappelton glowered, his voice and indeed his very countenance greatly transformed in the light of Croall's revelations.

'Is that so?' the curator enquired placidly. 'Then perhaps you might care to explain why it is that the police have been examining claims of mail theft at the Stirling sorting office these past few weeks - almost as though someone had deliberately been tampering with the postal service in the hope of finding a suitable target for their criminal activities.

'Strangely enough, just as the investigation into this misconduct was beginning to bear fruit, it was discovered that one of the sub-postmasters at the office - who was recruited to the position only last month - has inexplicably disappeared without trace. A Yorkshireman by the name of George Gatland, who had recently relocated to the Stirling area in search of a new start... and who, according to detailed police scrutiny, had presented entirely false credentials in order to secure the post. And do you know,' he continued, his expression growing ever more intense, 'it strikes me that the strangest thing about the whole affair is that this Mr Gatland should disappear at almost exactly the same time as the Reverend Mr Chappelton mysteriously arrives at the Smith Institute one frosty Christmas Eve.

'So there you have it, sir. You aren't Sebastian Chappelton, and I'd be willing to wager this entire museum - if it were mine to gamble - that you aren't George Gatland either. So exactly who are you?'

Though the counterfeit vicar's expression seemed to have turned forebodingly malignant, he was shaking his head in awestruck approbation at his host's powers of deductive reasoning. 'I have to hand it to you, Croall - you really are a piece of work. I would have considered myself one of the best confidence tricksters in the business, and yet I find that you have managed to second-guess my intentions every step of the way. Much though I detest myself to admit it, I would be remiss if I did not commend your assiduousness.'

'I'm not sure whether I should be flattered or appalled by your admiration,' the curator replied, his voice eerily calm.

'To think from the result of one single misstep - I had not anticipated you contacting your son by telegram, when your written correspondence with him had been such a regular occurrence - that you managed to completely unravel my entire scheme is nothing short of breathtaking. Who even could have presumed that a parish vicar would have found the time to reply at this time of year?

'And a replica emerald, substituted for the genuine article which was returned to its owner before there was a chance that it could be stolen... that takes ingenuity. But to then go ahead with a grand unveiling, knowing that you were showcasing a facsimile exhibit, while obscuring that fact from the entire Burgh... well, that's nothing short of genius. Surely the Provost himself must have believed that the emerald in that case was the real artefact.'

'I thought it best to omit mention of it to Mr Christie,' Croall responded with detached composure. 'The fewer people who knew of the imitation, after all, the more persistent the illusion would be when the time came.'

'And yet you could simply have called off the whole event, and no-one would have thought any the worse of you for it.'

'Cancel our keynote event of the year? This is the Smith Institute, sir! As I'm sure our illustrious founder would have agreed, the show must go on!' There was a glint of devilment in Croall's eye that was making Chappelton feel increasingly uneasy. 'The tenth anniversary celebrations went ahead, the grand unveiling occurred exactly as the Burgh Council had intended... and the opportunity was seized to apprehend a group of unprincipled thieves who, left to their own devices, would only have gone on to target

214

another establishment if this particular avenue of opportunity had been closed to them.'

'Besides,' added Kidston obligingly, as though completely unaware that he was in the company of a hardened criminal, 'just think of the enhancement to the Institute's public profile as a result of these events. When the full story emerges, the Smith will be the talk of the region for months to come!'

'Robert, my dear fellow,' Croall muttered irritably - though by no means too harshly. 'You aren't helping the situation.'

Chappelton still wore an expression that spoke of his amazement at the curator's barefaced audacity. 'That boy, Buchan Morris... no doubt you were responsible for him being present near that hatchway too, to act as a witness to what would unfold.'

'Not that he had any idea I was aware of it,' Croall smiled in satisfaction. 'Nor did Annie, when she gave him access to our private quarters - just as I knew she would. Nobody appreciates the wisdom and resourcefulness of children the way that my daughter does, sir; I simply turned a blind eye to their little scheme. I am, after all, responsible for the upkeep of this entire building: do you really expect that I would be unaware of what was going on in my own family's kitchen?'

'And yet by my reckoning there's one thing that doesn't make sense, sir.'

'*One* thing?' asked Kidston in bewilderment. Not for the first time, his utterance was ignored.

'When my erstwhile colleague faked his own death, and Engelmann pronounced him deceased at the scene, it was *you* who suggested that his body be stored in the boiler room. As you said yourself, you know every inch of this place inside out. So why on earth did you recommend that he be deposited in the only other part of the Institute with an exterior doorway? Surely you must have anticipated that he would escape.'

Croall laughed lightly. 'But of course, sir! That's precisely why I advocated that particular course of action in the first place. True, Engelmann had emptied the contents of the faux Major's pockets in front of the other guests... but it seemed a safe bet that one or both of his co-conspirators would have the means to either pick or otherwise break through the padlock, which would then allow Campbell to leave the building.'

Chappelton, the very epitome of dangerously strained politeness, was still looking confused. 'But... why? You could so easily have kept him contained until the authorities arrived to take him into custody.'

'And what would have been the point in that?' the curator enquired politely. 'Stealing a worthless replica emerald, even with all the trouble that you and your colleagues went through to obtain it, is one thing. But as he would have believed it to be the genuine article, I had hoped that your friend - the bogus Major - would attempt to trade it on the black market. Somehow I very much doubt that when the *objet d'art* in question was discovered to be forged, endeavouring to sell it - most especially to the sort of people that you presumably deal with - would have been advantageous to his career... or indeed his general wellbeing. Besides, with the heightened public awareness of the artefact, it may well have aided the police in tracking your group's activities: potentially even assisting them in shutting down your associates in the criminal underground, to prohibit such activities in future.'

The supposed clergyman nodded appreciatively, in the manner of a guest praising his host's choice of tea-cakes. 'I must admit, it *is* a very convincing forgery. Your work is to be applauded, Mr Kidston.'

'The pleasure is all mine, sir,' the mineralogist replied smoothly. 'Though I must say, it was one of the more unusual requests of my scientific career.'

'Besides which,' Croall added, 'you know as well as I do that the self-professed officer had no intention of waiting around until the police arrived on the scene - or, worse still given the nature of his ruse, the army. The real Major Campbell is less than amused at having been impersonated, given the importance he places on regimental honour.'

'It still seems, to me at least, to have been a gamble with unfavourably high stakes,' the one-time vicar muttered guardedly.

'If he was acting alone, perhaps; he may have grown desperate, his actions unpredictable. But - you will correct me if I am wrong, sir - surely that was the whole reason why you were present at the event: to act as a diversion, if necessary. Your partner in crime would have thought nothing of breaking a window to effect an emergency escape if he felt forced to, though given the need for circumspection I surmise that to be very much a last resort. I simply smoothed his path a little, to avoid endangering the guests. In any respect, like Engelmann you were on notice to cover for his flight from the building at any point - and to make it seem as convincing, or as confusing, as possible.'

'I'm afraid the truth of the matter is rather more mundane,' Chappelton smiled humourlessly. 'Someone had to be on hand to assist Engelmann with removing the body from the crime scene. If another party had been involved - Mr Baker or Mr Adam, for instance - they may have discovered that the Major was not nearly so deceased as "Dr Schottler" had pronounced him. And so I, too, had my part to play in the scheme.'

Digesting this information, though seeming less than surprised, the curator inclined his head quizzically. 'I had assumed as much. After all, why else would you have exposed yourself directly to danger in the way that you did, rather than simply pulling the strings from afar?'

'We were all agreed on the roles that we were required to play. And as the Bard tells us, are we not - at the end of the day - merely players on the stage of life? What happened to my associate at the Tay Bridge, no-one could possibly have anticipated... but he knew the risks involved in our line of work all too well,' Chappelton reflected gravely. 'Engelmann, on the other hand, paid the price for his hubris. Perhaps if he had spent more time studying his cover story - as I had repeatedly told him - his obfuscation may have had greater effectiveness. All he needed to do was think of some reasonable excuse to examine the body and, in the blink of an eye, he could have been gone via exactly the same route as our colleague. But in the end, he ran out of time *and* options.'

'Not so in your case, however,' Croall mused. 'I had a feeling that you would wait things out to see how the incident resolved itself. Because, if we are to be entirely candid, that is the only reason why you have remained in Stirling these past few days: leaving too early might well have aroused suspicion, especially when your face - and both of your assumed identities - would still have been recognisable to witnesses in the event of a manhunt, should your true intentions ever have come to light.'

'Had you been in my position, sir, I very much believe that you would have similarly decided to lead from the front - as our late friend the Major may have put it.' The criminal's eyes were dark, his expression unreadable. 'Especially if you had even a remote inkling as to the identity of our intended buyer.'

'Perhaps so. And yet you were just on the cusp of disappearing back into the shadows again when my missive arrived at your hotel... and then, just as I suspected, the potential risk that I had uncovered your true identity must surely have been outweighed by the nagging allure of learning just how far my investigations into your felony had gone.' His stare turned ever more penetrating, as though drilling into his guest's very psyche. 'I believe it was none other than St Peter who observed that even a pig which may appear spotlessly clean might still prove unable to resist the temptation of returning to wallow in its favoured mud-hole. Background research for a similar crime in the future, perhaps?'

Chappelton shrugged, his smile wolfish. 'As the scholars say, sir, research is everywhere. But frankly, I care little whether Engelmann is left to rot in a British prison or a German one - as far as I am concerned, he is a liability who has long since outlived his usefulness.'

'Indeed?' the curator asked mildly. 'You speak almost as though the same fate does not await you, sir. No doubt you are aware of the seriousness of the penalty which comes as a result of intercepting Her Majesty's Royal Mail.'

At that, the false clergyman allowed himself a chuckle. 'Mr Croall, I have enjoyed this fireside chat immensely. However, I presume that you are attentive to the fact that you have no chance of apprehending me.

'I must inform you, sir, that in my time I have cut throats, poisoned the innocent, and even throttled people with my bare hands. So while I have no wish to injure your feelings, I hardly consider an ageing curator and a weakling scientist to be much of an impediment to me simply walking out of the front door.'

'Quite honestly, Mr Chappelton, I feel that your summation is entirely accurate,' his host allowed graciously. 'Not being as young as I once was, I would hardly be of much use in a fight with an experienced criminal of your stature, and - as you rightly say - Mr Kidston here may have an exceptional mind, but is far from a hardened pugilist. However...'

Croall leaned over to the fireplace and rapped his knuckles loudly on its hearth three times in rapid succession. In the general hush of the reading room, the sound reverberated around the walls, the echo carrying out into the foyer beyond. Chappelton's eyes darted around the room as he leapt to his feet, clearly anticipating what was to come.

Sure enough, mere seconds later he could hear the clatter of heavy boots on the flagstones out in the entrance corridor. At the far end of the library, bordering the main entrance to the Institute, three uniformed police officers paced into the room. Clearly they had been waiting diligently in the curatorial office on the other side of the entrance vestibule, silent and out of sight, for the very signal that Croall had just given.

221

Burly and scowling, their adaptive stance seemingly ready to outwit any possible attempt to circumvent them, two of the constables had their truncheons drawn while the other was brandishing a set of metal handcuffs with no small amount of fervour.

At the other end of the room, a strangely ethereal figure was stepping forth from the shadows of the foyer, his emergence like a Sherpa appearing out of the mountain mists. Another member of the constabulary was pacing into the reading room - and, from the insignia on his epaulettes, he substantially outranked his colleagues on the other side of the library. The man was of average height, though wiry and compact. His eyes were sharp and alert, a snowy moustache and hair greying at the temples in no way detracting from the fact that he looked ready to spring into action just as quickly as an officer half his age. From his consciously unhurried pace and the overt confidence of his movements, Chappelton knew only too well that this man meant trouble; he gravely doubted his ability to best the policeman in a fight, fair or otherwise, though he was still mentally calculating the odds of being able to outrun the senior officer if need be.

'Mr Chappelton,' Croall announced cheerfully, as though making introductions at a dinner party, 'might I present Intendent McNeish. I understand that he has a number of questions that he would like to ask you.'

Knowing that he was now all but impossibly cornered, the erstwhile vicar shot Croall a look of pure malice.

'If you would care to follow me, sir,' McNeish said dourly, his comportment making it clear that Chappelton had no option in the matter whatsoever. 'I would require you to join us at the station as part of our enquiries.'

Chappelton shook his head in disappointment at this turn of events, though it was apparent that the curator interpreted the gesture as the over-emphatic affectation that it so clearly was. 'A pity, Mr Croall. Had things been different, I could have made you a rich man. But rest assured that even if it takes me years to achieve it, I will make this Institute pay for the inconvenience you have caused me here today.'

'A rather grand ambition,' Croall responded flatly, 'especially for one who may not be seeing daylight for some considerable time. Goodbye, Mr Chappelton. May you fare better than your colleagues.'

'I intend to, sir,' he sneered vituperatively. 'I most certainly intend to.'

The Intendent was advancing, slowly but surely, on Chappelton's position, his subordinate constables watching their superior's movements closely. 'I can assure you that you will have plenty of opportunity to talk in the very near future,' McNeish said ominously. 'But in the meantime, I must ask you to...'

Only then did Chappelton made his move.

Croall was visibly startled at the speed that the criminal was able to manoeuvre, his monochromatic clerical garb making him appear like a magic wand in flight. Chappelton shot past McNeish and darted into the foyer before the officer could even begin to lay a hand on him.

'Mr McLafferty!' yelled the curator as he rose from his chair. 'Stop that man!'

The Intendent was already blowing his whistle, though the gesture seemed entirely superfluous as his junior colleagues were actively in the process of filing back through the far door in an obvious attempt to intercept the absconding criminal at the entrance vestibule. Croall and Kidston, on the other hand, were hurriedly following McNeish through to the entrance concourse... when they were all momentarily stopped in their tracks by the sound of a bloodcurdling scream.

Stepping through into the concourse, Croall's eyes widened in surprise when he discovered the source of the disturbance. There, suspended midway through the revolving door, was Chappelton - his left leg, still in the foyer, trapped at a rather unhealthy-looking angle. Any attempt that he may previously have made at frigid composure was now completely undermined by the look of sheer agony that was spread across his face as he dangled halfway through the doorway, his flight to the building's entrance painfully curtailed. On the other side of the revolving door, blocking Chappelton's exit, were the three constables, each patiently waiting for the criminal's release from his temporary ensnarement. Any hope that the escaping felon may have had towards circumventing McNeish's officers was now hopelessly thwarted.

'Capital work, Mr McLafferty!' the curator cried in triumph. 'A palpable hit. It seems that you have saved the day!'

'Just daein' my job, sir,' McLafferty sniffed modestly. 'As Milton tells us, "they also serve who stand and wait". And a timely reminder, if I may say, of whit happens to those who think they can sneak oot without having paid the entrance fee.'

Kidston winced, unconsciously checking his pocket for loose change.

'Alright, gentlemen,' McNeish said, the starkness of his tone chilling the sanguine levity of the moment. 'Allow me to take things from here.'

* * *

Chappelton's bruised dignity seemed to have taken the fight out of him by the time McLafferty released the criminal from the door. The Intendent's men squandered no time in handcuffing the felonious non-cleric, and appeared to take great pleasure in making him limp painfully along the entire length of Dumbarton Road as they began their journey back to the police station in the heart of town.

'One may have thought that the Intendent would have summoned a carriage,' Kidston mused from the Institute's grounds as he and Croall watched the entourage of lawmen disappearing into the distance. 'Mr Chappelton - or whoever he really was - seemed to be in no fit state for a long walk.'

'No, I suppose not,' agreed the curator, his breath frosted in the chill air. 'Which, I imagine, is precisely why a carriage was *not* summoned.' He withdrew the replica emerald from his pocket, holding it up to the morning sunshine as he examined the stone in all of its multifaceted glory. 'Such a beautiful object, for all its material worthlessness. It rather saddens me that we will most likely never see the genuine article now.'

'Pfft!' Kidston snorted nonchalantly. 'If you've seen one emerald, Alexander, you've seen them all. Now fossil spores - that's a *real* field of interest. Did I ever tell you about the time I spent at the...'

Croall let his zealous young friend continue in his account for a moment or two, though his own mind was elsewhere. Kidston was unquestionably an exceptional talent, and the brilliance of his observations usually offered up some nugget of interest or other, but for the time being the curator was simply content to enjoy the freshness of the cool winter morning and the quiet chatter of squirrels as they chased each other in the tall branches of a nearby oak tree. The Institute itself stood silent in the watery sun like a sentinel, its grand portico dominating the curator's line of sight. *Five years open to the public*, he mused reflectively. *Whatever will the next five bring?*

'If anyone ever tells you that curatorship is a dull business, Robert,' he said suddenly, 'you may with confidence call them a liar.'

'Decidedly so,' Kidston nodded pleasantly. If he was surprised by the abrupt interjection, he showed no sign of it. 'But if I might ask, my old friend, what do you intend to do with that would-be emerald of yours? Not that it is worth a great deal, I grant you - but after the events of the past few days, somehow I doubt that it will bring back particularly happy memories for you or the Institute.'

Croall paused for a moment, looking in silence at the faux gemstone and casting his mind back over the chaos that it had caused. Should he return it to Kidston as a memento of his scientific ingenuity? Or perhaps it should be lodged in the museum collections, an idiosyncratic curio for future generations to ponder upon. Then again, given the amount of trouble that it had already been responsible for, the easiest course of action might well be to melt it down and try to forget that the whole sorry course of events had ever taken place.

'Do you know,' Alexander Croall said finally, 'my office has long been in need of a paperweight of reasonable quality. Though I may have come to it by a very circuitous route, I do believe this little chap will fit the bill perfectly.'

And so it did.

227

CURATORS AND CUSTODIANS
OF THE SMITH INSTITUTE
(NOW THE STIRLING SMITH
ART GALLERY AND MUSEUM)

Alexander Croall (1874-85)
James Sword (1885-1922)
Joseph McNaughton (1921-48)
A.J. Taylor (1948-49)
Robert Moffat (1949-55)
Robert and Bessie McLeish (1956-57)
Miss Hunter (1957-58)
Mr Dalrymple (1958-59)
James Thomson (1959-80)
Michael McGinnes (1979-)
Deborah Haase (1982-89)
Pamela Diamond (1989-93)
Dr Elspeth King (1994-)

AFTERWORD

BY DR ELSPETH KING
DIRECTOR OF THE STIRLING SMITH
ART GALLERY AND MUSEUM

This story, based on a fictional huge green emerald, is a work of literary imagineering conjured by Thomas Christie from little scraps of fact and historical information, drawn from the Smith Institute's past. I hope you have enjoyed reading it as much as the crowdfunding supporters have done.

The book is important for the Smith and Stirling. As Alasdair Gray said in his novel *Lanark* (1984), no one can imagine living in a place unless it has been written about or has featured in novels, poems and films. The Smith is almost 140 years old, and has had a slow start.

In 1994, Stirling Literary Society, who have held their monthly meetings in the Smith for 24 years, commissioned the play *A Scenery of Dreams* by Neil Scott to accompany the Robert Louis Stevenson Exhibition. The play is set in the posthumous afterlives of Thomas Stuart Smith and Robert Louis Stevenson, and highlights the likelihood that Stevenson used the dramatic elements from the life of Smith in his story *Kidnapped*.

1998 saw the 20th century edition of *Blind Harry's Wallace* published by the Smith and Luath Press, followed by Lesley Duncan's *Wallace Muse* in 2005.

In 2001, James Robertson published *Stirling Sonnets*, featuring 16 items in the Smith collections and, in 2011, Alistair Findlay's poetry collection, *Never Mind the Captions*, featured a number of objects in the Smith.

In 2010, Bloody Scotland, the annual meeting of Scottish Crime Fiction Writers began in the Smith. In 2013, the Smith's own work of crime fiction, *The Shadow in the Gallery*, was written. Author Thomas Christie has given super-sleuthing powers to Alexander Croall, the eminent natural historian who was the Smith's first curator, and has extolled the dedication of David Buchan Morris, who grew up to become Town Clerk of Stirling and a Smith Trustee.

However, it has been the administrators of the Smith in the past twenty years who have rung the changes. Thomas Christie, in his 15 months in that post in the Smith, set up the Smith's first dedicated website, secured a substantial Smith entry in Wikipedia, produced nine YouTube films, a set of leaflets on Smith history and raised money to replace the disabled lift, whilst carrying out the day-to-day management. He has now produced a gem of a book for Stirling and the Smith, which will be polished in the creative writing sessions planned for the Smith's 140th anniversary.

Dr Elspeth King
Stirling, 2013

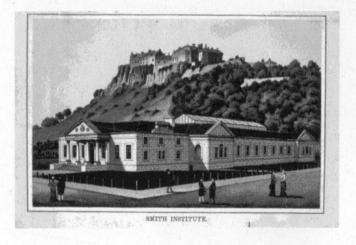

SMITH INSTITUTE.

The Smith Institute

ACKNOWLEDGEMENTS

There is an old saying, as true today as it was when first coined, that books don't just write themselves. While this may well be an accurate summation of the craft, it is a fact every bit as correct that even the most solitary of authors rarely write a book alone. It is to this end, then, that I would like to thank everyone who has offered me a benevolent word of advice and constructive support during the time that I've spent researching and writing this novel.

My gratitude goes to my wonderful family, Julie Christie and Mary Melville, for all of their kindness and patience during the writing process. Thanks also to my good friend Professor Roderick Watson for many a fruitful brainstorming session spent chatting over a hot cup of coffee as we discussed both fiction writing and Scottish history. I am greatly indebted to the Reverend Dr Adam Hood of St Andrew's Wallace Green Church of Scotland, Berwick-upon-Tweed, for his kind advice regarding the ecclesiastical issues of the Anglican Church during the late nineteenth century. My gratitude also goes to Eddy and Dorothy Bryan, Sarah Fletcher, Ian and Anne McNeish, Dr Colin M. Barron, Alex and Kelley Tucker, Lesley Duncan, and Denham and Stella Hardwick, for all of their friendship and kind words.

I would like to offer a special word of thanks to everyone at the Stirling Smith Art Gallery and Museum for their lasting fellowship as well as the very detailed information that they provided during the research for the book. I am especially obliged to Michelle Cook, Michael McGinnes, David Smith, Margaret Job, Vincent Connell and Michael Donnelly for their time and help right throughout the whole cycle of planning and developing the narrative of the text. However, I would like to reserve particular gratitude for the help of the Stirling Smith's Director, Dr Elspeth King. I am thankful not only for her advice, support, sharing of ideas and historical detail, but also for her invaluable books *Old Stirling* and *A History of Stirling in 100 Objects*, both of which were enormously beneficial reading material during the planning of this novel.

To everyone who has offered their time and friendship during the writing of *The Shadow in the Gallery*, thank you one and all.

ABOUT THE AUTHOR

Dr Thomas Christie served as Administrator of the Stirling Smith Art Gallery and Museum between the summer of 2006 and the autumn of 2007. In that time, he made many lasting friendships and forged a relationship with a great institution which has endured ever since.

An elected member of the Royal Society of Literature, the Society of Authors and the Authors' Licensing and Collecting Society, he holds a first-class Honours degree in English Literature and a Masters degree in Humanities with British Cinema History from the Open University in Milton Keynes, and a Doctorate of Philosophy in Scottish Literature awarded by the University of Stirling.

He is the author of a number of books on the subject of modern film which include *Liv Tyler: Star in Ascendance* (2007), *The Cinema of Richard Linklater* (2008), *John Hughes and Eighties Cinema: Teenage Hopes and American Dreams* (2009), *Ferris Bueller's Day Off: Pocket Movie Guide* (2010), *The*

Christmas Movie Book (2011) and *The James Bond Movies of the Eighties* (2013).

Tom also writes in the field of literary studies; his book *Notional Identities: Ideology, Genre and National Identity in Popular Scottish Fiction Since the Seventies* was published in 2013.

For more details about Tom and his work, visit his website at: **www.tomchristiebooks.co.uk**

FURTHER CROWDFUNDING THANKS

With appreciative thanks to everyone who so generously pledged funds to the Stirling Smith's crowdfunding strategy of 2013, an appeal which was administered by Michelle Cook and Dr Elspeth King with the aid of the *Crowdfunder.co.uk* website. Sincere gratitude goes to all of the following people, each of whom helped to make the publication of this novel a reality:

Anonymous, Amanda J. Baker, Eddy A. Bryan, Elma Cheetham, The Cook Family, Anne Patricia Cunningham, Stephen Daglish, A.I. Dickson, Alexandra Dobson, Kevin Douglas, Steven Douglas, Alan Douglas, Elizabeth Douglas, Lesley Duncan, Mitchell Earley, Alex & Mary Galloway, Grace Goodwin Smith of Fintry, Stella and Denham Hardwick, Judy, David Kinnaird, Isla, Ian McNeish, Michael McGinnes & Lesley Botten, Matt McGrandles, Susan Mills, Ian Milton, Alex and Patricia Neish, Elspeth O'Brien, Colin O'Brien, Hilary O'Donnell, Karen Smallman, Grahame Smith, The Stewart-Earl Family, Joseph Weir.

So you think you know the full story of *The Shadow in the Gallery*?

Think again!

Visit the book's official website at

www.theshadowinthegallery.co.uk

for exclusive bonus content including:

- Discover the inside story of the Smith Institute's celebrated first curator
- Learn how the nineteenth century helped to shape modern Christmas traditions
- Who's Who in *The Shadow in the Gallery*
- Victorian parlour games and festive recipes
- Alexander Croall's guide to the Smith Institute
- And many more surprises besides!

Visit the Location of
The Shadow in the Gallery!

The Stirling Smith Art Gallery and Museum
Dumbarton Road, Stirling, FK8 2RQ
Established 1874

www.smithartgalleryandmuseum.co.uk

Open to the Public
Tuesday to Saturday: 10:30am-5pm
Sunday: 2pm-5pm

ADMISSION IS FREE

For further information about visiting the Stirling
Smith, including guided tours and educational
visits, please call 01786 471917 or e-mail:
museum@smithartgalleryandmuseum.co.uk